The Marriage at Antibes

fiction

Carol Azadeh

CARROLL & GRAF PUBLISHERS, INC.
NEW YORK

First Carroll & Graf edition 2000

The author wishes to acknowledge James Fox's *White Mischief,* from which she drew inspiration for the Kenya material in "Bronagh."

Grateful acknowledgment is made to *Conjunctions* in which "The Country Road" was published.

Carroll & Graf Publishers, Inc.
19 West 21st Street
New York, NY 10010-6805

Library of Congress Cataloging-in-Publication data
is available.
ISBN: 0-7867-0708-9

Manufactured in the United States of America

to Mamad

Contents

the country road

On the quiet country road I stopped. The warm air moved among the seeding roadside grasses nodding their blobs of cuckoo spit and the bitter blackberry bushes coated with road dust. I was walking up to the pub and willing something to happen. Now. Make it now. Then I had to slow down because the pub, Keegan's, was getting farther behind me and the mulberry bushes of our lane coming nearer and the rule said that the magic held as far as the big stone outside our lane. *Now.* And in that split second, the sky opened behind me and roared past, screaming dustily, sealing my eyes and lips in dryness and fear and joy at my power to call forth an event. When I was able to look, I saw a motorbike, the driver whooping freely; behind him flowed dark brown hair, sleek and long enough to sit on. 'Celine,' I gasped. The bike swerved, made a round dust-whirl and, before leaping into our lane, paused infinitesimally, just long enough for me to understand with my middle child's percipience that

Celine on the back had not wanted the bike to turn off thus, she did not want Mammy stumbling out of the kitchen into the hen-yard to see her eldest daughter on this bike with its dark green mudguards and brake shield. I ran all the way down the road to our lane, my school bag bumping up and down against my back, my sandalled feet slapping against the lonely quiet that had closed over their passage. In our lane they had flung the bike against a hedge; in the sunlight and smell of warm tyre one of the wheels turned slowly. For a moment I stared—they had tricked me! I crouched on the grassy verge, dropped my school bag, gently parted the hedge and white-weed, resisting the powdery, itchy smell of the whiteweed ... and then I stopped. I knew enough and so much by simply closing my eyes and seeing how her long, thin brown hair covered her back and his arms that to this day I can't tell if I saw them there in the quiet field or not.

This was the nineteen-fifties, and the countryside of the north of Ireland was quiet, inhabited by Sunday sluggishness that thickened in the vein. Not many people could afford to put a car on the road. I was a schoolgirl and I had lived nothing but that road on past the schoolhouse and our lane. Just after the school the road turned at Biddy Dempsey's shop and went on into town past Keegan's pub. Old hairy-faced Biddy Dempsey had a wild temper. On Saturday afternoons my big sister Celine and her friends walked idly past the shop, looking in the dim window and commenting loudly, daring each other to obscenities and laughing at the top of their voices until Biddy flew out, shouting at them, hairy face and bony body clenched and shaking with anger like an impotent Rumpelstiltskin, and the girls ran off shrieking with half-simulated fear. (I remember Padraig Pearse laughing and calling me Biddy Dempsey for screaming in rage.) By the year I was eight, Biddy had lost her sting, her face had sunken in on its gummy toothlessness, eyes and mind had rheumed over. 'Biddy's winding down,' said our daddy. So there was no longer any crack for Celine in walking past the shop door, arm in arm with her best friends, to taunt the reaches of Biddy's anger straining like a dog on its chain, and I knew Biddy would no longer tell on me to Mammy that summer when I defied the hawthorn stick on the top of the kitchen press, and to the pace of my hard-beating heart walked farther up the road than I was allowed by myself, past the riverbank of long grass, on to Keegan's pub with its wire-meshed window of tea-coloured glass and the dour plank door painted brown.

There I paused, waiting for someone to go in or out. On the afternoon air I breathed the smell of fry from Biddy Dempsey's dinner until hunger got the better of my trepidation. In those warm spring afternoons the road slumbered. The fields released their pre-summer smell of turned clay, thick bruise-coloured clouds insulated the earth. I waited, watching the plank door of the pub, and when Biddy's lunch faded there came the forbidden, sickly sigh of beer-on-the-breath familiar from visiting uncles.

The door stayed closed, blank, its painted slats of wood changeless as the small green fields on either side of the road.

These were the months after my eighth birthday. Every afternoon after school and before tea I ran back down the road towards our lane, hungry, but light-footed and light-hearted too at running alone on the road, the breeze in my hair and my school bag bumping against my tailbone, and then Mammy's face, heavy, wary with fatigue, rose before me. Mammy rarely left our cottage. She was as permanent a fixture as the pump under the hedge which dealt us our water. When our daddy wasn't home, Mammy shivered at movements in the yard outside. In those winters before electricity came, black dark drowned the country from shore to shore. Mammy huddled in the oil-lit three-room interior of the cottage like a big fragile insect stuck on a lamp.

Already at the age of eight I swore never to cower like Mammy. After supper I liked to announce that I was going out. Roused from her bleariness she said, 'Houl on, let me look,' and went slowly over to the kitchen door to check the incoming dark. If she didn't catch my arm I slipped by her, wee titch, being light, unlike Mammy, and free as a bird. I ran off, laughing cheekily in the night air, pounding my feet on that dusty lane with its high spine of tufted grass. I had a coal-black cat called Pusheen, a flighty, susceptible animal who followed me bounding madly like a dog, ears flat on its head until it dived into the hedge, overcome by its own excitement.

Mammy called me her 'changeling'. She wanted to excuse my scrawny, sallow-skinned limbs to visitors who admired the other rosy, plump children, good-looking by country standards. The tone in which she said 'changeling', pinching my 'tinker-brown' skin or catching my eyes in the mirror when she was combing my hair back into the severe plait I hated, made me laugh. When at last, at night, Mammy sat down at the kitchen table, she never suspected how I studied the quiet in her eyes or looked at the width of her back and hips straining over a pile of sheets in the washbasket and wondered, 'Is she really my mother?' Or perhaps she did know, which explained her tendency to take the hawthorn to my legs more than she did with my brothers and sisters. Those days Mammy beat me absent-mindedly, breathing sterterously, more out of duty than anger.

One evening in the spring of that year Celine and I had been clearing the table after dinner when Mammy told us to stop and listen to her. Then she said baldly that from now on neither one of us two, nor our younger sister, were allowed up the road past the pub by ourselves.

'Why not?' I demanded instantly, knowing I couldn't rely on Celine, who was too sly for direct opposition. Fourteen-year-old Celine had just earned the right to Saturday dances in the town hall and would henceforth submit to anything to keep that privilege. For the girls like Celine in those days, the girls who grew their hair long to compensate for a plain face and paid no attention at school, life melted down to Saturday night, which in turn dissolved into the single hope of getting a dance from a boy with a car.

'Because I don't like you girls going past that Keegan's pub, that's why, and because I say so,' said Mammy.

Poor Mammy. 'Thick' was the word for Mammy, for the pre-mature obesity of her arms and legs from cooking all day for the six of us, 'thick' the slowness of her head from standing on her feet from dawn to dusk every day, 'thick' her inability to explain herself to herself, still less to her children. When life was beyond Mammy, she made a Novena to St Jude, Help of the Hopeless, getting up even earlier than usual to go down on her knees. Mammy did not tell us a new B Special barracks was settling in the market town that began at the far end of the road. That is, she set out to tell us about it, she had been turning the words in her head all day. But St Jude worked a miracle of transubstanti-ation. Old, well-established anxieties, Drink-Fear, Pub-Fear, absorbed the new fright of B-men and what they might do to her girls, and finally with sustained prayer the whole anxious mass coalesced into the reassuring threat of the hawthorn stick.

My sister and I looked at each other wonderingly. We thought of Mr Keegan, whom Mammy said was 'a soak' and 'you could smell it on him a mile off', and Mrs Keegan, a bony, cross woman never lit by a smile. I saw Celine's one-track mind thinking that the only men around Keegan's were toothless, propped on sticks with the sky in their eyes.

Mammy caught my eye. 'I mean what I toul yez an' don' let me hear of yez wanderin' up there on your own,' she threatened, suspicion turning her intolerant. As always our big brother Padraig Pearse, whose loud, brash manner was law in the cottage when our daddy wasn't there, backed her up.

'The road's not for wee girls,' he sneered. 'The road's not for titchy girls,' he said.

From that day on if Mammy ran out of sugar or tea, she sent out Padraig Pearse. And that's what got me thinking about Keegan's. That's how the pub's wire-meshed square window turned into a blind eye whose mystery I determined to pluck out, and I began walking up there regularly after school.

I walked that road in all seasons. The surface patched with tar was as familiar to me as the changing patterns of healing scratches and bumps on my knees. Rain, warm or cold, sleeked the tar and ran into pools in the cowprints trodden on the clay verge. On bright days the distant whitewashed walls of cottages like ours caught the sunlight on the violet slopes of the far hills. I walked alone. Celine and Padraig went to the senior school in town, the wee ones played at home all day. Sometimes a tractor roared past slowly, leaving a trail of straw and diesel in the field-scented air. Or a bicycle, bowling elegantly against the breeze. Then the quiet closed over my head, the country quiet, the wet quiet of a clay burial. I liked to imagine myself from the viewpoint of the other driving or cycling past me, a thin, bushy-haired girl in a green felt cap walking alone no one knew where. I tried to forget that later the very same day they would probably meet my father in the fields round about and say, 'I saw your wee Cathy on the way ti school today.'

Later that spring the weather turned hot. Patches of the road softened in the heat. I picked off the small lumps of pitch stuck to my shoes and rubbed the tar-stains with butter. I invented ways to keep the tension in my defiance of Mammy as I walked up the road after school, forbidding myself to breathe or even look at the pub until I came to the long grass opposite, but boredom got the better of me. I was no longer interested in the pub for disobedience's sake, and my feet trailed heavily on my way past the wire-meshed window. The day that I saw Mrs Keegan get out of a car and go in with another man was going to be the last afternoon I bothered walking so far down the road. A missionary had visited the school that day and told us about Signs of Christ revealed, including photos of Canadian snow melting in the form of Christ's face and a vision of the crucifixion formed by blood-red clouds at sunset. So I was paying attention to the sky. The usual heavy rainclouds ranged the horizon. Behind them rolled the sun, piercing their weakest places with beams that shone on the arable earth in straight lines like the Holy Ghost illustrated in my school catechism. The man with Mrs Keegan was a stranger, poor and from town by the look of his thin trousers and battered sports shoes and dark, floppy hair. Men like my father wore heavy work-shoes and cut their hair short. This man couldn't even afford light town shoes.

'Hullo Mrs Keegan!' I sang out instinctively from the other side of the road.

'Hullo there, wee Cathy.' The sad-faced woman scarcely glanced over at me. Dark Floppy Hair did not turn his head. He took keys out of his pocket, unlocked the pub door and stepped back to let her pass before him. With the plank door opened, the foreign, stale smell of spirits that so terrorized Mammy sneaked onto the road. Mrs Keegan went in first, without looking behind. The unembellished door closed behind their backs.

It was Padraig Pearse who picked up that word from neighbours who came to our cottage with the news. Celine and I were hanging sheets in the back. I couldn't remember having heard the word 'rape' before but it didn't surprise me. Now I knew the mystery of the wire-meshed window. Masked men had burst into Keegan's pub, 'the very time wee Cathy was comin' home from school', sighed Mammy thankfully, crossing herself and promising St Jude a Novena and also St Anne, the Blessed Virgin's mother. They had tied the publican up in a cupboard and raped his wife before shooting him through the cupboard door.

'They put a towel over his head,' said Padraig to Celine where they sat on the doorstep, keeping an eye on me as I played dressing up Pusheen in dolls' clothes before wheeling her around in the rusty baby's pram. A baby's game which I hadn't played for a long time but today I felt like bossing Pusheen, whose wiry black body arched angrily against my hands as I forced her to the old humiliations of dolls' bonnets.

'They raped her,' Padraig Pearse said to Celine, who was

examining the curtain of her hair for split ends.

'I know,' said Celine without asking what that meant.

'They gagged him.' My big brother had the same disgusted emphasis he had heard adults use. 'They cut off all her hair too.'

Celine's green eyes gleamed wide. 'Why'd they do that for?'

Padraig Pearse shrugged. 'The Keegans a been keepin' house for the B Specials in that there bar. She'd been goin' wi' them. They do that to them girls that goes wi' the B men.' The righteous tone sounded odd in his mouth, for at fifteen years of age he still hadn't made it his own.

Home, schoolhouse, home, chapel, home. Patience was the smell of a rain-soaked, sun-beaten road. For eight years I had breathed the light-pink and dark-pink tea roses proliferating on our cottage walls. Inside smelt sweet and suffocating, of cinders and baking and damp and soap, like a fat grandmother pressing you to her chest, summer and winter. Every morning and evening we fetched water from the pump, Celine and I. When winter came on we lit the oil-lamps early. In summer we lay in our bed wide awake because night refused to come and the sheets smelt damp from the chill of the stone walls. At night the country silence deepened, submerged in darkness. The sound of a dog barking carried on the still air, then stopped. Sounds disappeared in the night leaving echoes to fade like the ever-widening circles after a stone thrown in a deep pool. Cast-iron was that winter quiet. I remember lightless winter afternoons lived under a white monochrome lid, fields, road, trees, stiffened into voicelessness. At last with spring the movement of green differentiated this silence. Cottage doors opened to the pale sun. The first grass smells in the quiet hinted at long summer days outdoors from dawn to sunset for which the air was still too chilly. We were impatient and restless, we hungered for summer. The first signs of real oncoming heat were the pink scent of the opening tea roses, the flies being hard to keep out of the cottage and then the old people who had survived winter and came visiting in the spring. They sat by the fireplace distilling that faint odour of piss and cheap *eau de toilette* that I have come to associate with illness or old age. Their gossip was of lawsuits over bits of land, of men and women broken by marriage and drink, of cancer, deformity, accidents, decapitation, bone-breaking and attack from farm tools and animals, as if their bleak words could tempt providence to compensate them for the hard times of old age in an unforeseen stroke of bad luck. They did not spoil us or try to win our love; we had to be on our best behaviour, even Padraig and Celine, and not do anything they might report in other cottages. Mammy gave them the best to eat and drink while they commented that we were 'wild eaters' and 'surely stout ones to feed', and finally I remember that often we couldn't bear to look at them. They were ugly with hard gums instead of teeth and pushed-in faces and rheumy eyes and the sight and sound of them eating a plate of stew was enough to put you off your food for a week. And yet our daddy said that they were not much older than him, only their lives in the fields had been backbreaking. He added honestly that we were lucky not to have to share the cottage with an oldie, thinking of his unmarried sister who lived alone with an aged aunt 'who ruled the roost' and from whom she was to inherit the house and the piece of land it was on.

In the spring of the year I was eight I saw our daddy stand

for a long time in the doorway in the evenings and stare at the high sky ribbed with the soft herringbone clouds of reluctant summer, so as not to have to listen to the old men in the firecorner. The next morning at breakfast he sucked in his cheeks toothlessly, screwed up his eyes and nudged Celine.

'D'ye mind that aul bull of O'Hearn's and the times I toul yez that it were a dangerous beast that should be put down?'

I spluttered into my glass of milk.

'Catch a hold on yerself,' Mammy said crossly, coming to set the teapot on the table. Mammy never understood our daddy's jokes, which she considered a sort of side effect of what she called his 'moodiness'. *He's a shockin' moody man.* When our daddy mimicked the neighbours like this, Mammy always imagined that it was me leading him and the others on. It had been years since she loved our father as well as she loved her eldest son, Padraig Pearse, the only one of us humourless enough to batten on her admiration.

'Sure there was I in broad daylight in Market Street wi' my wee gran'son Jimmy,' our daddy went on wheezily, 'an' that great beast come chargin' round the corner up ti Jimmy and knocks him down flat on his back before continuying on up the road and away on, on outta sight, as if nothin' a happened!'

'What about wee Jimmy?' said Celine, who could keep a straight face.

'Sure, he'd no idea what an' under God had hit him, it happened that fast! I goes inti the nearest shop for help but none of them ones believes me! For the aul bull has gone and wee Jimmy's jumped up saying he's as right as rain! I ask ye, after being toppled by a great bruthe of a bull like O'Hearn's! "Niver mind yer saying yer right as rain now," says I to Jimmy. "Shut yer face an' come down to the police for I'll witness against

O'Hearn's bull and have him for trauma if it's the last thing I'll ever do!"'

'Cathy!' Mammy snapped.

Our father wiped his mouth and stood up. ''magine the traumytizing effect on a child of being knocked flat by a bruthe of a beast like that!' he said to Mammy above the delighted shouts of the two wee ones infected by the covert glances and smiles of Celine and Padraig. 'Enough to ruin a child for life, do ye not think, Eileen?' he murmured, going out the door.

'Go on the rest of yez, scat,' said Mammy, 'I'm at the end of my tether with ye all!'

When I was eight I really thought that this was all that would ever be. These long, daylit, amorous evenings of late summer (I didn't know the word at the time but the softness of the pinkening summer days already caressed me into a state of anticipation nearly unbearable), and the image of a sunken, toothless mouth chewing on itself, which I tried not to look at. I was first one home from school and I ate the grilled potato pie that Mammy had ready on the stove. I argued with Mammy about going outside again while she forced me to do some useless housework for which she had no time, polishing brass ornaments, rubbing stains out of sheets, ironing Celine's frilly dance dresses. I spent the end of the day alone with Pusheen, playing in the yard while the shadows coagulated around us. I always pretended not to be waiting for our daddy to come back from the fields but I was waiting, waiting. His return was the only event in the evening and, finally fed up, I finished my day in a fugue of ingratitude. Just as her cat-spirit soared ecstatically in the half light, I tapped Pusheen smartly on the nose, which she hated so much that with a back-flip and a yowl she vanished into the shadows.

Everyone knew our daddy's comings and goings were the peaks and troughs of my days. Sometimes today the warm grass smell of a daylit summer evening brings back the peculiar flavour of my waiting for him that year when I was eight. I stood at the mouth of our lane, smelling the flourishing hedges which scented the air like a caress, watching the expiring heat rise to the lilac sky. After a certain period of waiting and seeing no movement on the road between Keegan's roof and our lane, bleakness settled, large, damp and ugly, like a big insect fluttering in the centre of my being, and my heart began to beat uncomfortably in time to the idea, *What if he doesn't come* ... . I stared dully in front of me as if the air were grey, the fields naked brown and the sky blank as a dead dog's eye. Those were moments I'll remember until the day I die, the dull moments of being eight and lonely on an isolated country road. A dullness worse than anger, worse than crying, and the reason why, even to this day, and although they'll never understand me, I can never take my own daughters back to the country, or tell them they are right in the romantic country tales of my childhood they have invented for themselves in their heads.

What if he doesn't come ...

Our daddy would appear without warning, striding along noncommittally as if he had been there all the time on the road before me. If he saw I was in a bad mood, he stopped and opened his arms. I ran to him and then the whole of that day, the trepidation in my heart of sneaking up to Keegan's, my defiance of Mammy, the dullness of waiting, the terror that he might never come, all melted in the certainty that my time of light-footed happiness would come true as surely as our daddy swinging along the road to meet me.

It was to him that I complained, especially when Mammy did not let me go outside after school, that 'all the days were the same'. If he was tired, he reacted with a grain of Mammy's 'thick' wisdom. 'Stop your whingin', darlin'.' More often he didn't answer but picked me up and set me on his shoulders (showing he, like the rest of them, thought of me as a baby, though more fun than the wee'uns). 'Titch, wee Titch,' our daddy said when I was angry and screamed at Padraig, who liked to boss me around, 'What are ye so mad at?' Padraig, not understanding our daddy's tone, joined in, jeering, 'A great big voice for a wee titchy girl!' They all laughed, Padraig Pearse loudly, just to hear himself, Celine silently, squeezing up her green eyes and pushing back her sleek, dark-brown hair, which she never forgot was long enough to sit on, and Mammy with her tired, gamey smile because she always thought Padraig's loudness was funny, and then the wee brother and sister who didn't know anything but always watched Celine's and Padraig's faces to understand what to do.

That summer our daddy came home from town with an oval radio in polished nutwood which he placed on the mantelpiece where it watched us like an owl. Mammy smiled slowly as she always did at our daddy's ideas. The wee brother sucking his thumb hid behind the wee sister. Celine looked at Padraig, who disguised his curiosity and asked cheekily like a big man of the world, 'How much'd that cost ye then?'

I knew then I was justified in loving uniquely our daddy in this family. Apart from me, only he understood how the radio's urbane chat banished the clay silence of the fields, the awful bleakness of their retained breath in winter, the suffocation of their moist fertility in summer. 'A circle of good company,' he said, which meant the news from Belfast at six and London at seven and an alternating rhythm of something different through the bedroom door left ajar at night and also in the afternoons when I played in the yard which smelt of cows, baking bread, buttercups and rose petals. Between us we knew that he believed in an alternative to that endless beat of day following on day and season on season, timelessly without change forever and ever world without end, Amen.

After the radio came the visit from our uncles who lived down south. We knew that they had come to talk seriously about an old plan in our family, the dream of emigration to America. The brothers, Barry and John James, arrived up from Dublin. They gave us children money as they always did and sat back gravely around the fireplace, which smoked with a damp summer fire out over the hearth chock-a-block with flies leapfrogging round the stains and remnants of pieces of bread and cake eaten there and hard bits of food thrown into the embers. The uncles smoked too, thin packs of Players with a red stripe. They let me scratch their unopened packs to find the place where the gold band tore evenly round the wrapper like a present. These men smoked so hard their fingers were mustard-coloured from the third joint upwards and their clothes smelt so raw of smoke and sweat that Celine, who stayed outside or in the bedroom practically all the time they were there, put her finger down her throat to make fake puking motions behind their backs. I was still young enough to have their dry, hard hands on my head or even around my waist while they talked and I fiddled with things from their pockets. I had to be there with them, and not just for their unwashed, sweaty smoke smell that as the hours went by absorbed into itself all our smells from soap and baking powder and fry from the kitchen and even the old, deep fugs and scents of the fire. I couldn't resist staying there, listening, through Mammy's comments on how spoiled I had got, through their long dull hours of talk, because since the brothers' arrival our daddy's new, strange vivacity changed our house more than Christmas, more than I had ever believed it was possible to change.

Mammy had cooked a special meal of stew under pie crust to 'see off' the brothers' return to Dublin. That night we were to finish the big, baked dome for dinner but the meat and potatoes in the centre of the table congealed in their glass oven-dish. Our daddy, usually first to pile his plate again, had laid his knife and fork across his plate, meaning he could eat no more. His excitement curtailed our appetite and bothered Mammy into the beginnings of her usual fearfulness.

'My stomach couldn't take another drop of food tonight,' he stood up, his hand light on Mammy's shoulder, then he left the kitchen through the halfdoor closed all day to keep out the hens. We saw him walk across the moonlit yard with his hands in his pockets. Mammy looked at Celine and started to cry. I didn't take much notice; she cried so often, Mammy, sometimes out of sheer tiredness, and even then I thought that was her own fault. No one *asked* her to work that hard. The story was that the brothers, John James and Barry, planned to emigrate to New York the following winter. December, January was a good time. Our father would follow with me, then send for the wee'uns and then my mother with Padraig Pearse and Celine. Over the next weeks, the family split down the middle. Behind our daddy's back, Padraig swore he would not leave the country. He had just finished school and he envisaged a year or two dossing as a farm hand, drinking, flirting in the fields around the cottage. Celine said nothing. Nevertheless, I knew from her smile and her narrowed eyes she was with Padraig. At fourteen she had tasted too much of the local dancehall to be tempted by other freedoms.

In the days after the uncles went back to Dublin I took advantage of Mammy's frequent tears to leave the kitchen without bothering to clear the table or waiting for her to send me out to the pump for dishwater. Outside in the yard, Pusheen, a long black stain in the moonlight, scampered like a firefly against the cottage wall. I chased her briefly and then wandered over to our father who stood smoking at the start of the lane up to the mulberry bushes. Already I was sure America would be everything we both wanted. I knew myself wiser and older than the others behind us in their kitchen, fearful in their warm meat smell. Our daddy put his arm around my shoulder, one hard hand on my back.

I looked at the sky. Above the arable fields the white-ribbed cloud plains held the dark.

'America's like the sea!' I said to him. The night air on my face smelt of grass and the warmth of the animals who had lain on it all day, an odour so etherealized by the wind and the moon I could smell salt in it. I realized then that the joy that had been in me since the moment in the kitchen when he had stood up and walked out was like the shock that had hit me last summer when we rounded the corner in the bus at Castlerock and saw the sea, oblivious and contained and more real than any picture I had ever seen. He laughed, then sighed and rubbed his hand over his face, 'I don't know, I don't know.'

'I have so been to Castlerock last summer!' I reminded him, irritated by this drop in his spirits.

'And ye wouldn't miss home and all?' he asked me in a strange tone.

'All what?' I turned to look at his face, sombre and handsome (as I remember it) in the moonlight. He indicated the end of the lane which ran into the Wee Field pitted with heel-shaped ridges, small wells the cows' hooves had left, now filled with reflecting water. A solitary thorn tree, scraggy and well known by day, stood transmogrified by moonlight. I was thinking only of how, living with him in America, with Celine and Padraig Pearse staying behind, I would be freer and happier than ever I had been in my whole eight years.

'What's there to miss, we're all going together!' I said. He stroked the top of my head and then stood up slowly.

'You should've been the eldest boy.'

At night he took a chair and, placing it outside the front door, sat with his legs crossed, gazing straight over the field whose darkness held steady to the depths of the moonlit spaces overhead. Mammy made me go to bed earlier than usual, which I did without fighting; our daddy's mood had cast a peculiar spell on me. In the dark bedroom where my sisters slept peacefully, I smelt the smoke from his Player's No. 6. I left the bed where Celine had rolled heavily into sleep and tiptoed to the deep-set window. The thick little pane we never opened magnified the starlight. I clambered onto the broad sill and saw the dark effigy of his head. The stone under my legs was colder than ice. Lifeless, intractable cold under which nothing grows; not even in deepest summer did those stone walls ever warm at the centre. I climbed off, found a towel, spread it on the sill, and with a secret shiver of delectation settled back, determined to keep vigil with my father in this night so precious in its miraculous advent of a new world. The novelty of my happiness accentuated every detail around me. I was living the happiest night of my life and I knew it. Never before had I been aware of the grandeur and the sorrow of passing time. I stared at the sky fretted with constellations whose names I didn't know, not understanding this emotion for which tears seemed so inappropriate. The immobility of the stars, their infinitesimal winks in the quiet sky worked on me until their silence filled my ears with a single symphonic note ... Yet his head motionless as carved stone, the monotonous rhythm of his smoking, broken now and then by his thick cough, a sound to which we were all so used that we scarcely heard it any more, lulled my eyes. I heard his monosyllabic replies to Mammy's concerned voice from inside the yellow of the kitchen and at last I slid sleepily off the sill and went to bed just as Mammy, always nervous and deferent to our father's 'moods', shuffled tiredly to rest herself. I knew that Mammy was thinking, 'Ah, I'm weary, weary, so weary,' and my last thought on that strange, luminous night of happiness was that Mammy had never bothered to understand our daddy because she was always too tired.

I was putting Pusheen's front legs through dress sleeves when I heard heavy boots skidding down the lane and dragging a weight behind in a skittering wake of pebbles and dry mud. Before I had time to look up Mammy rushed out of the cottage with her hands to her face, shouting at me, 'My God, my God, wee Cathy!' Her voice trembled. Later on, the memory of this pathos made me angry; what was I supposed to do to assuage her helplessness, her beseeching me to contradict the sight before us?

Two men held daddy under the arms and dragged him roughly into the house as I remembered once seeing them heaving one of my uncles home down the lane after a Christmas dance in town. That had been on a crystalline night in January and our daddy standing in the oblong light of the doorway had laughed at their ragged songs and the scarves of their misty breaths in the air. Today, the sun brightened in the sturdy monotony of mid-afternoon. I squeezed Pusheen, who scratched my forearm before streaking treacherously behind me.

His face was limp and his head slumped as if someone had cut the cords in his neck. I ran up to him and saw a shining, white line between his half-opened eyelids, then I knew that he was alive and I grasped the sleeves of his hanging ragdoll arms and pushed the men's legs away with all my force.

'Nobody asked you lot to come here, let him go!' I screeched at them, throwing myself on him where they had laid him on the bed. They pulled me off at once, quietly, saying, 'Would ye take the wee'un, Eileen.' Mammy's trembling, disorientated hands pushed me out of the room. Nevertheless, pressing my face to my father's neck I had already had time to smell the rubbishy odour of his breath which shocked me to silence. I had never been close to rot before and didn't know the name of the sweet smell in my nostrils.

The men bringing our daddy back from the fields had seen him groaning, crouching over a stone. He was vomiting blood in the first of the haemorrhages from the stomach cancer that meant instead of starting life in a new country, he was going to die at the end of the summer, at the age of forty-one, in the ancient familiarity of the three-roomed cottage he had lived in all his life.

Rape was an eyeless, noseless maskface, a heart beating in a dark cupboard, a wire-meshed window, an explosion of light and sound in the tiny space of the head. At night I lay awake, hugging the wee sister for comfort, and watched Celine sleep with her hair over her face. In the day a fleeting, sickish smell lined my nostrils; I couldn't tell what it was until I remembered Mammy's disgust for Mr Keegan—'Did ye smell it on him? Sure ye could've smelt him a mile off!' Then I knew I had the death smell of whiskey in my nose. I dreamed I sat alone in the middle of a sticky floor in the shade of Keegan's pub and the battered sports shoes appeared before me. It was Dark Floppy Hair with his gunflashes who said, 'Where'll I kill ye? In the feet or the head?'

I screamed with cowardice and reached for a soft body beside me for protection, the wee sister, whom he killed easily in a vertical line of bullets; then bullets spat, neither hot nor cold, along my legs.

After our daddy's death I used to dream that my screams woke him up and brought him into our room. 'Whisht, will'ye quiet up wee Cathy! It's only a bad dream!' Celine shook me awake. 'Look, there's Pusheen!' The black cat had sensed my wakefulness and turned in the pinkening square of the bedroom window, opening her mouth in a silent plea. Celine, freed by our daddy's death to drop out of school and work backbreaking hours in a shoe shop in town, fell asleep again instantly. I lay awake and thought of how daddy's forehead wrinkled when he was tired, how he rubbed his face pretending to be sleepier than he was when he wanted us all to let him be. What if I asked him where Mrs Keegan was now? Gently he said, 'Sure, I couldn't tell ye.'

Of course we didn't go to America as he wanted us too. We went on living at the bottom of the grass-ridged lane dense with mulberry bushes, in our three-roomed, whitewashed cottage. The thick stone walls trapped flies and clammy heat in summer and preserved the damp chill of winter. His death had weakened me. The power of the year when I was eight faded in the oncoming seasons. Then I was only a child growing up, her fantasies no longer strong enough for the magic of calling an event into being, as I had once conjured Celine on the motorbike coming home from school. After my daddy's death I started to faint regularly. I fainted in mass and at school, so often that the nuns stopped paying any attention when it happened. We went on living together, Mammy, Padraig Pearse, Celine, and the wee'uns who had no memory at all of our daddy's plans, and no suspicion, when Mammy took the stick to their legs, that the wrong one had died. She didn't hit them as hard as she had beaten me, though. Tragedy had sealed her into a sort of hopelessness which irritated everyone except Padraig. Unlike the others I argued with Padraig every day. I could not be like Celine and agree with one side of my face whilst doing what I liked with the other. I screamed at Padraig because although he was only my brother, Mammy's docility allowed him the power of forbidding me to leave the cottage in the evenings. At fourteen I took to spending my days like an old woman, glowering at visitors from my stool near the uneven stone sill of the kitchen window, or staring out at the lane that led to the main road behind the mulberry bushes. I didn't say a word to anyone but I was waiting to go away.

One day near the end of those years Padraig Pearse refused to allow me to go to a local *céilídh*. That is, he swore he would come and 'make a show' of me in front of the whole *céilídh* if I 'dared' go out of the cottage that evening. It was the height of summer again, the time of pink evenings, flies and tea roses. I was 'thran' for not wanting to stay off school and 'help out', which meant cook for everyone. Mammy had been in bed, feverish and sickly as she was more and more often those days. She blamed her ill-health on her teeth. This time she had, in fact, been speechless with toothache for nearly a week.

I waited in my usual seat at the kitchen window. Behind me summer flies piled stickily in the cold grate. Padraig helped Mammy into a neighbour's car he had borrowed to take her into town to the nearest dentist. I watched them, my Mammy and my brother, as if they were people I didn't know. Though she was not even fifty years of age, Mammy's back was hooped from hardship. Her teeth had browned and gone rotten in her gums. Near the car door, she turned and hesitated in that mute manner that always irritated me. She held on to her son's arm, peering anxiously at my face in the window. Since our daddy's death she didn't like any sort of venture into town by car or bus. Her sheer recalcitrance before trips to the doctor or the dentist stopped up my pity for her. She had tied a scarf round her neck and the pain in her jaw prevented her from saying anything. Padraig slammed the car door behind her and followed her glance in my direction. Under his breath he swore and called out, 'Don't you dare budge from the house, wee

Cathy. We've some talking to do when I get back.'

I didn't answer. I didn't 'budge' until the car had climbed the lane leading up the hill to the main road. Even then, with my eyes closed, I could see the rough grasp of his hand on the arm of the old woman who swayed slightly at her son's loud words.

People I don't know.

I left the cottage, taking nothing but my cardigan and a pocketful of biscuits. I stepped out of the muddy farmyard pitted and ploughed by goat and cow hooves, walking quickly, not looking back at the tiny white cottage behind me. In the summer heat I walked over the fields to our 'neighbour's' farm. There I slipped into an animal shed and stole a bicycle. I intended to ride it to a chocolate factory near Castlerock where I had heard they were taking on packers.

The summer day burned hot on the tar of the country road. All my life the smell of melting tar will remind me of this flight to freedom through the full-leaved countryside mature in summer under the high sky, nearly the high, magical blue of my first childhood. I was happy. Not the eight-year-old height of joy, but happier than for a long while. Blackbirds plunged madly across my path into the thick hedgerows. In the rush of the bicycle I was mistress of myself at last. Once I had arrived in town and found a job, I would be an adult. Padraig Pearse would never be able to make me come back to the cottage. I sang into the field-scented air.

The route I was taking wound circuitously uphill and down, looping around fields and thickets. My back and legs did not begin to ache until long after I'd left behind me the houses and shops after Keegan's. Then I lost all sense of time. Sweat clouded my vision, weariness numbed my feet. A sweetish late afternoon enveloped the town I was riding into and I cycled past workers hurrying along the street. The chocolate factory would be closed for the day. My only desire then was to stop pedalling but the constant motion had mesmerized my legs and so I continued, cycling round the streets where shopkeepers were stowing boxes and crates and locking up their shops. In my head, a chill space of fading brightness, there beat mercilessly the winging rhythm of bicycle tyres on the grey road that chilled in the rising night. I would have ridden the stolen bicycle until I had dropped off, if a car had not emerged unexpectedly from round a corner and knocked me flying over the handlebars. Pain split diamond-hard in my head. I fell into the dark.

Someone repeated my name. Warmth soothed my forehead, an insistent acrid smell drew me up to consciousness. I resisted. Lost and resisted again and slept. 'Cathy, Cathy,' said a voice I recognized. I opened my eyes. They had laid me on my back on the grey sofa of a small shop storeroom. From stacked cardboard boxes came the disciplinary tang of antiseptic. The softness on my forehead was Mammy's weak hand stroking my hair back from my face. The old woman's touch shook. I had frightened her. Tears oozed helplessly from my eyes. At that moment Mammy's trembling struck me as the most unbearable sight of all. I closed my eyes again. 'Don't,' I said, lifting Mammy's warm, dry wrist away. 'I'm alright.'

'How is the wee'un, Mrs Kelly?' came a voice from the back of the shop.

'A'right, 'hank ye'ery much, Mr Mawhinney,' said Mammy. From behind my shut eyes I sensed how she turned her head gratefully in the direction of the voice. Her voice sounded thick, as if with tears. But when I opened my eyes again, she was looking down at me, smiling. My heart froze. Mammy's mouth was a swollen weal. And something else. Too soft, boneless, a mimicry of a mouth, a cheeky hand in a sock mimicking a gummy old woman's mouth. For the first time I noticed the bloodstained white cloth in her shapeless hand. 'What did they do, Mammy?' I cried, turning my head violently on the grey cushion of the sofa. It was her teeth. They had taken out the rest of her teeth.

'Ssshush up, wee Cathy,' said Mammy. 'They gave me some stuff so's I don't feel a thing. Don't fuss yoursel'now.' The thickness of her speech against her soft gums did not hide the satisfaction of a buyer who has made a bargain. 'Sure I'll be a new woman the morrow.'

They took me back to our cottage in the neighbour's car. Padraig driving had nothing to say, after all. His head was an inert rectangle turned to the road from whose green-black night midges and moths and every other variety of summer insect flew headlong against the windscreen. Mammy dabbed ice wrapped in a pink-stained cloth to her face with one hand and tried to restrain my tears with the other.

Even now, when I haven't been back along that road for twenty, thirty years, I remember how I wept all the way home through that summer night while Mammy dabbed her mouth. I remember how I was weeping, not only for the exhilaration of my flight that had dissolved like the memory of sunlight in the night, but also for some other inconsolable defeat which would take its toll, even when I flew again. Overhead, the stolen bicycle tied to the roof-rack of the neighbour's car shifted back and forward with the movement of the car. The accident had only twisted the front wheel a little. It would take to the road again. Slightly, slightly the wheels moved in the animal-scented air that stretched for fathoms over that black country.

bronagh

In Spain Bronagh had just turned twenty-three. At Cambridge those who knew her had feared that her tense, perfectionist character and a bad first love affair would bring on a nervous breakdown, but she had sailed through top of her year in mathematics and physics. Her tutors were predicting a career in research, maybe for some government institute or in the embryonic computer industry or subsidized research in the States. When she hesitated, then went on an ill-advised teacher-training course, as thousands of young women were doing in the mid-sixties, they sat back and raised their eyes to heaven and washed their hands of her. The girl had always had an odd streak. It was her life. After the training course Bronagh couldn't bring herself to apply for teaching positions because surely life couldn't go full circle so quickly. Something else had to happen before she turned into one of the teaching instead of the taught. So she borrowed the keys of a small villa near Granada. The villa, called Media Luna, in the village of San Gines, a *pueblo blanco* lost on the Andaluz hill-lands and ignored by most tourist guides despite its ruins of a small Roman aqueduct, belonged to the family of Monty, a friend from university. He warned her that the electricity in Media Luna was 'ramshackle' and that there were cockroaches in the kitchen, but still his tone of voice as he spoke was unmistakably envious. 'The heat there goes right over the hundred-degree mark in summer and there are pools of ice-cold spring water you can swim in.' The idea was that Monty would get away too and join Bronagh; he was now doing his novitiate in a City job he hated but was good at. 'Say your fiancé's on his way out,' he said and laughed, for he had just moved in with another young man with whom he described himself as perfectly happy in a flat in Knightsbridge. To Bronagh's surprise, apart from a massive picture of Marlon Brando in *A Streetcar Named Desire* they had stuck up on the bathroom wall, Monty and his young man were filling their home with the heavy, valuable, light-devouring furniture her own mother would have chosen. But then Monty was never one of the free revolutionary children of that implausibly accelerated history of their time, the age of exploded hydrogen bombs, men in space, Ho Chi Minh, JFK, civil rights sit-ins, independence riots. 'Say your fiancé and his brother are on their way out to see you, that'll reassure them,' he told Bronagh. 'They're a bit behind, out there in San Gines. All their interesting people have gone to Paris or been garotted by the *generalísimo*. Better take a pile of books for company.' Bronagh lied vaguely to her mother about looking out for teaching work in the south of Spain, about meeting a female friend from college there, then packed, including her sketch-books and paints. She herself knew well she had acquired too much of her mother's anxiety about what constituted real work ever to take her small talent seriously enough. Still, maybe ...

Then, in Spain, in San Gines, she got very unexpectedly happy, in a simple, safe way proverbially associated with childhood, and this was why although twenty-three she considered herself at last in the morning of her life. There was no substantial reason for her happiness. At night, with the heat of the day gone into the grass and the black sky, she sat up late drinking a few glasses of red wine at the tables in the village plaza with a book propped to ward off unwelcome attention. After a few laborious conversations about its being easier to read in the café at night than in the electricityless villa, the locals left her more or less alone. The café was one of the few buildings in the village with reliable electricity and running-water facilities. She loved the smells of the night air, the fried butter and stale cheap wine of the café, the tobacco and Moroccan hashish mingling with the conversation around her and the music from the radio behind the bar. By two o'clock in the morning the café had emptied out, the radio had been turned off, the night air in the plaza, freed from the scent of tobacco and alcohol, was clean as water. Sleepless, peacefully adrift like a balloon cut from its moorings, Bronagh walked back to the unlit villa on the hill. She was happiest of all in the mornings, which came only a few hours later. Her eyes opened in the southern light that until midday accorded even the humblest wooden chair, cracked cup or scraggy tree the purity of line and form, the intensity of snowy white, viridian and azure, that must have first suggested to human beings the idea of some other perfect lost state, and now at least reminded adult senses of childhood. This was the light of Bronagh's earliest childhood. She had been born in Kenya and lived there until she was four, when her parents separated. Then her mother had taken her back to the coastal town where she herself had spent her girlhood, a plain semi-circular seaside resort in the north of Ireland with a convent school on a promontory overlooking rainswept dunes. The Irish Atlantic was to Bronagh a place of greys and browns. Their flat on the harbour was full of covered furniture, of dark wood primitives that her father had stored meaning to sell off one day, along with Thika hunting trophies and photos of roy-alty visiting the coffee plantations.

In the villa Media Luna Bronagh lay clearheaded, gazing for a long time at the luminescent patterns on the porous white walls and ceiling. She got up, washed and dressed, avid like a child for the day to begin, parted and pulled her hair to one side in the loose pony-tail she had worn all her life, tugged on her shoes and left the villa to go and buy the first bread. Light of foot, her long, spare body exhilarated by the sunny morning air, she sprang from the verandah through the gates of Media Luna, which could not be closed for they had sunken off their hinges and rusted into the ground in an open position. On those mornings on the chalk-white road into the village, a promise of celebration came out of the quiet, out of the smell of damp earth, the slow noises of animals being moved for feeding or milking, the vastness of the pale, shiny sky. She would sleep off the weariness of her legs and arms in the heat of the afternoon. In the fields tanned sheepskins were strung for drying in the bright wind from North Africa. She ate a bread roll or bocadilla with butter and cheese, had a café cor-tado and smoked her first Ducados of the day. For company she had Pilar, a primary school teacher who had taught herself English because she liked it, speaking surprisingly well for someone who said she only talked to the rare tourists passing through San Gines and only wanted to understand the Beat-les. Pilar had read Hemingway from the university library in

Granada. Bronagh lent her Virginia Woolf and George Eliot. Pilar abandoned the first because the sentences were too hard to understand and 'too ladylike', but she approved of George Eliot and spent a month with all her dictionaries out reading *The Mill on the Floss*. 'You don't have to ask how I like it, you see I am reading non-stop.'

'Why not travel and use your English?' Bronagh put to her.

Pilar shrugged and laughed. 'Why travel? Why not stay here and read books and meet you who come all the way to San Gines?' Her prettiness came from her healthy smile and also the energy in her dark grey eyes under a heavy fringe. Her hair was long over her shoulders in the plain, schoolgirl style of the time. She was slim but strong, her hands hard, her arms and legs muscular from farm work. At the school where she taught she wore a long dark skirt with a leather belt and flat shoes. When she had been working on the farm she wore trousers cut off below the knee and the same leather belt. Like Bronagh she usually wore no make-up. Whereas Bronagh's face looked scrubbed, ascetic around the fair-lashed eyes and fine, pale lips, hers appeared sparkling, full of movement, like a faceted gem in the light. Pilar's skin was paler than most of the villagers' but in soapy water had the buttery evenness of southern skin that would turn brown in the sun. Bronagh liked her at once; Pilar was the most glowing, frank, good-natured person she had ever met. She came to the villa to take baths because the house where she lived with her family did not have a bathroom. In Media Luna the bathtub was porcelain, on claws in the middle of the room, and Pilar lay happily with her long hair lifted over the edge like one of Renoir's young women at the beginning of the century. *La Baigneuse*. An ancient posture, thought Bronagh, its lines probably an ideogram in some ancient language, an Egyptian hieroglyph. Bronagh, who couldn't read or draw in the combined heat of the bath and the Andaluz summer afternoon, lay on a punctured sofa against the wall opposite the windows and fanned herself with one of the dusty painted straw fans she had found in a drawer.

'Oh yes I will travel of course,' said Pilar. 'Maybe it's good to go for a while to a big city or another country and then come back.' She flexed her toes on the opposite rim. 'I don't know. You see I see always advantages on both sides of a question. This is my problem.' She laughed. 'It doesn't matter! I am not like you, obliged to one true answer only. Full of sorriness. Sorry-ness.'

This last referred to the meaning of Bronagh's name in Irish. *Tá bron orm*, I am sorry or sorrow is on me. 'Get it off you then!' said Pilar aflame, half-scoffing as in everything she said.

'It wasn't me, it was my mother,' Bronagh protested, feeling silly because Pilar began laughing again as if she was hearing exactly what she expected to hear. 'She wanted some typical Irish name.'

Sometimes Bronagh thought Pilar was as young as seventeen or eighteen, and at other times, when she found herself the butt of Pilar's irony, as old as twenty-six or twenty-seven. They had taken bottles from Monty's family's cases of alcohol hidden in the cellar, gin and whisky and vodka as well as wine, concentrating mainly on gin because there were two cases full of Gordon's and Bronagh remembered Monty saying it was as cheap as the local red wine out here and thus easier for her to replace when she left. Occasionally Pilar brought beer.

'Cold beer. It's the best,' she said. 'Why do we like drinking so much?'

'Because we know God doesn't exist,' Bronagh said.

'You are wrong. Alcohol is for talking.' She laughed. 'For believing what you say and do nobody has said or done before.'

'That's God's illusion.'

'No, that's the illusion of my father.' She hardly ever brought her family into the conversation and Bronagh always refrained from asking her questions on the subject although there was nothing about Pilar she didn't want to know. 'It's talking in the wind, this beer,' said Pilar sombrely. 'Making nothing that lasts.'

They wanted to drink red wine but they would attract too much attention buying up wine supplies in the village. Or busing it from the nearest big town. This was a country where the population was supposedly united by religious dogma, by the law-givers, a place where you could not live publicly as you liked. Monty had described with his usual narrative flamboyance how fathers in the haute bourgeoisie dutifully took their sons to brothels to ensure an initiation that would immunize them against homosexuality. Contraception was not available except on the black market, condom smugglers had recently been acquitted of raping teenage tourists who sought out their services, and there were the atrocity stories from the civil war, of which each pueblo had its share, since the white mountain towns had provided footholds and hideouts for anarchists and socialist sympathizers.

'What can we say, we know it happened,' said Pilar when Bronagh asked her about stories like those of the gorse-filled gorges not far from San Gines into which the Spanish Africa Legion had tossed live prisoners, 'yet it's difficult to believe that we are ready to rip each other like rats imprisoned in a cage which is too small for them.'

Pilar took Bronagh to a pool Monty had told her about, between boulders and scraggy bush growth outside the village. They swam there in the hottest evenings, despite the mosquitoes, and when there weren't other villagers picnicking or locals larking on the dessicated grey-white boulders under the trees on the banks. Pilar said the pool was fed by a lake where swimmers had drowned in hidden whirlpools, but the pool itself was safe. A mysterious aqua green floated in its depth as if some jewel or stone were dissolving there. These were the days before industrial pollution dyed Spain's rivers stinking purple and yellow. Swimming was best when 'pleasantly pixilated', as Monty put it, with local red wine. Or when Pilar's brothers gave her some shit for a joint, though Bronagh once got a mild eye infection from floating stoned and open-eyed on her stomach over the fuzzy shapes of small, pallid rocks on the pool bed. Pilar made fun of her red, swollen eyes from which pus wept for two days.

'Oh Bronagh you are so ugly! I can't look at you!'

'Why didn't you stop me then?' snapped Bronagh. 'You were there too, you saw me.'

Pilar had been lying on her back, eyes closed, with her head on the musty edition of *The Mill on the Floss* which Bronagh had taken from her mother's bookshelf. On the flyleaf was written her mother's married name, Grace Wycherley, Kenya 1942, the year of Bronagh's birth. From time to time Pilar had raised her head and flung bits of twigs and pebbles at Bronagh floating face-down in the pool, arms adrift like a drowned person.

'You must know that water's not one hundred per cent clean,' said Bronagh irritably. 'There may have been a dead animal or something in it.'

'Oh yes. Surely water-rats,' Pilar concurred. 'You can see them at night yourself.' Her eyes opened wide in amazement at Bronagh's anger. 'But Bronagh,' she said half-laughing, 'it's not my fault! I was there but I was out of my head too!'

It took Bronagh a long time to understand that this was how Pilar was healing her, by returning her to the middle ground where blame, like anger, appeared not only pointless but ridiculous, risible. Once she had grasped this, her admiration for Pilar knew nearly no bounds. Slowly her careful taciturnity gave way. In the summer heat, when haze settled suffocatingly on the country outside Media Luna, there was not much to do except talk. All the windows thrown open wide day and night created the only most imperceptible of air currents and the crannies and crevices of the walls and floorboards were colonized like the rest of the house by the crickets, spiders and ants that had made the matted and tangled garden their own. Bronagh and Pilar sat upstairs in the room with the bath. By midday, and until four or five in the afternoon, the flaking shutters pulled to a convex V created a convalescent dim against the heat turning white over the earth. Apart from the freedom Pilar created naturally around her, the relaxing ritual of a bath, the soothing, absentminded water movements over her submerged body lulled them like oars dipping in a slow river. For the first time, Bronagh surprised herself with the strength of her confessional instinct, along with the intense gratification involved in making someone laugh as Pilar laughed, her eyes sparkling, watching in vivid and ironic detail the scenes called up by Bronagh's words. She listened with interest to the details of Bronagh's childhood, describing her father's visits from Kenya to the flat in the seaside resort of Portdoran—occasions when Bronagh was not allowed to come to her mother's bed in the middle of the night even after a bad dream (this last made Pilar laugh). Like Bronagh, Pilar smelt his cigarettes in her mother's clothes, the soap in the steam of his baths, the scentlessness of his freshly ironed clothes. She saw the pale lipstick Bronagh's mother wore then. Pilar too listened to their voices from behind the closed door across the hallway, witnessed the conversation always closing quickly round her mother's comments and suffered all the old stories he told about his famous temper. How he had masterminded the notorious episode when Lord Cairsforth stacked a pile of brushwood around a government office in Nairobi and threatened to set it on fire if they didn't accord permission to set game traps in a wood on his land. How he scrutinized her mother like an old miser taking a piece of jewellery out of a scabby cloth and holding it up to the light.

'I can hear him now,' said Bronagh. She was sitting very still and her head was gently turned, a gesture she had inherited from her mother. 'As if he's in the room here now and the way he used to talk to her about me as if I wasn't there, *Grace, Grace, ignore her, you give in to her too much.*'

'Wait. She wants to see him too if she asks him to come to her house.'

'He's dead now,' said Bronagh. 'No, you're wrong. He made her do it. He brought people to Ireland for hunting, fishing trips, and she happened to be there.'

'They didn't take care about you having fun. Probably you had a lot of time for thinking.' Her eyes twinkled. 'But Bronagh, better to think of her enjoying, no?' She looked up, her even, white teeth on her lower lip, suppressing some word or expression. 'Was he good-looking?'

Bronagh thought of the deeply sunburned skin that had

appeared so foreign to them, the hard, bright beauty of the sun in those blue eyes, like the light in a chiselled jewel. A hunter's acuity and also some of the freedom of an animal. She said, 'Being out there all his life changed his looks. People say I take after him.' She thought of him looking at her in her mother's presence and saying, 'How old are you now? She must be my daughter because she looks like me.' And yet she's nothing like me, was the unspoken corollary, meaning her quiet, tense manner, her mother's lack of veneer in company. Also, Bronagh's childhood asthma had set her among the delicate, the friable, like her mother, who suffered from pains in her neck and back that she said came from the ill effect of the strong sun in Africa but which were in reality the legacy of the rheumatic fever she had suffered as a child. Bronagh said, 'He had a northern face improved by the sun.'

Pilar, luxuriating in the bath water, closed her eyes. 'Sun improves everything. I could not live without it. So, finally, she left Kenya. Not him.'

'I don't know,' Bronagh said. It was true. She did not know enough about human neediness and instinct and how the forces of history or society can pick up your life and set it down impersonally, and this sometimes without your even having realized anything had been going on. Their generation in the western world was both younger and more sophisticated than preceding generations. Not until years later did she have the experience to imagine the atmosphere her mother must have lived in and then fled from in the last years of British Kenya. The whites like her father, who supervised the houses, animals and Somali staff of the White Highlanders, would have been Home more and more often, smelling of sun and alcohol and talking of safaris and 'sundowners'. She imagined her mother's gentle struggle to hold on to the precepts of her Catholicism when her father had only derision for the religious, 'the Holy Joes in Lourdes who threw away their crutches and walked'. Her mother's inability 'to take alcohol', along with her timidity, her reluctance to seduce or flirt and keep up a front like other couples, her incapacity to intimidate African servants— all these must have been factors pushing her to separate what self remained from John Wycherley's lifestyle in Kenya and come back with her daughter to the place of her own girlhood in the decaying afternoon light of the north of Ireland.

Bronagh had a capacity for idealization and its opposite that had already nearly been her downfall once before, in that bad time when people were predicting her sombre, brooding attitude would put paid to her future. At the time she hadn't listened to other people's warnings. They didn't understand that it didn't matter she was allowing someone to take from her time, her peace of mind, in the end her sleep, her health. When they remonstrated she herself protested that the imbalance was temporary and would rectify itself.

Pilar did not need to take. Pilar was not needy, though she lived on an Andalucian farm with three brothers and two sisters. She enjoyed her work with children in the local primary school, for she knew that being with children at this moment in their lives she was doing something vital for which she would be remembered. 'This is more important than money.' Pilar's father had fought on the losing side and been imprisoned, probably tortured too, during the civil war. One of Pilar's brothers was in hiding for his sympathies with some anarchist movement. None of this was anything exceptional among the inhabitants of the straggling *pueblos blancos* where Pilar's family had lived for generations. Nevertheless, when questioned about her own politics Pilar displayed a circumspection that Monty would have applauded. 'This I can't answer because everyone knows this already. Everyone knows what is the big dream of this moment. Justice, equality.' Bronagh beheld Pilar's humanism, her *joie de vivre*, her intelligence in seeking out books and languages without caring a jot for the pat-on-the-back, the social esteem of academic competition. Her heart grew light at Pilar's nonchalance, her warm, gleaming eyes, her happy, healthy smile which showed she was supping experience from the brim. She felt amazed at this accession to a newer, freer life than the other lives she had left behind, infanthood in Kenya, then childhood in Ireland with her mother, school and university in England. Maybe more than one life is possible after all, she was thinking, if you have the courage to go after it.

When the evenings lengthened and grew as hot as midday, and in the front garden of Media Luna there increased the stridulation of crickets and other insect carpentry deafening at noon and after sunset, Bronagh often came back to Media Luna to find Pilar sitting smoking on the verandah. On seeing Bronagh, she had a habit of throwing the butt into the garden in an arc of indifference until Bronagh expressed her worry about setting the dry grass on fire, at which Pilar stopped smoking altogether. She said she was not really a smoker. It was a reflex from seeing everyone else doing it around her and then what was the need to smoke in a place so peaceful, with the smell of fruit and the earth, we were not office workers with their little tight chests that had forgotten the taste of clean air.

'How do you know, you've never been away from San Gines?' Bronagh tended to cut in on Pilar's rhapsodies of place. Especially since she had heard the civil war stories.

'Yes but this doesn't mean you can't like beauty, this is something that is not true,' Pilar rejoined in her heavy accent, looking up at Bronagh from the verandah steps. 'Anyway, where will I go? England is so cold, the pea-soup will kill me.'

'Pea-souper,' said Bronagh. 'You're thinking of Dickens' London. This is the nineteen-sixties. The fog has gone.'

'All those long-faced Virginia Woolfs on their park benches. Ireland drizzling, Scotland the same, cold, rain.' Pilar hugged her knees to herself. A piteous note entered her voice. 'If I go the States it's so far I have to emigrate. You can stay here with me, it's easier. Or let's go later together. That way you show me everything.'

'Alright,' said Bronagh lightly, not paying her words much attention; she was thinking how Monty would find Pilar too emphatic. They would not get on but he would forgive her because of his aesthetic snobbery. He would succumb to her healthy, sparkling prettiness.

They were drinking on the verandah of Media Luna, their naked feet side by side on the railing that looked out over the insect-drilled garden and the rusted gates open on the road down into the village. Bronagh was tired from wandering miles that afternoon in heat so intense it made her shiver. She had taken her sketchbook and gone into the scrubby hills behind the pool, but when she sat down to work the heat and brilliant light had drawn her inspiration out of her. Also, she had not brought enough water and was bothered by thirst.

Mechanically she copied thistle-like plants and silver-trunked trees. Brown ants with articulated waists kept overrunning her book and pencil. No shape or colour would come; her mind had turned to some doughy substance in which no matter how she pressed, not a form or mould would take. Pilar too had been out in the fields all day checking a watermelon harvest with her brother and sister, and she was still wearing her farm work clothes. In the beginning Bronagh had hoped to find an occasion to offer to work with Pilar's family too. She thought it would do her good to work outdoors and learn a new skill, to connect with the life of her infancy in Kenya where her father had been chief groundsman, though her mother never worked outside. Pilar, however, had not yet invited her to the house where she lived, 'my grandmother on top of ourselves, my brother and his wife on the other floor'. These last were people whom Bronagh could not even tell from sight among the other villagers at San Gines, so it hardly seemed possible to raise the question of work.

Since late afternoon a heat mist had obscured the distance in a whitish grey-blue. In this season the evenings either grew muggier until nightfall or, on days without cloud cover, the radiant blue sky invested plants and rust-coloured earth and even silvery road-dust with an almost unsustainable rippling brilliance succeeded by drifting, peaceful sunsets over the damp exhalation that since Bronagh's arrival was the only moisture available to the dry land. Pilar had come for a bath, but the glasses of Gordon's and the day's heat were making them lazy about checking the water cistern and the functioning of the electricity generator. Tiredness made Bronagh focus on irrelevant details. Pilar's feet, thin, supple with strong knuckles on the first big toes, were, like her face, her legs up to her knees and her arms to her elbows, a deeper shade than the rest of her body. Her own small, white feet, the toes bunched damply and effacedly together, were a cadaverous colour she tried not to look at. She was thinking as she did nearly every day that she still hadn't unpacked her paints.

'What do you want to do afterwards then, Pilar? I mean years after all this.'

'After? Oh you know first we girls in San Gines have her great duty to God, then we can think of something else.' Alcohol tended to disintegrate Pilar's grammar but this was her way of talking about marriage. Not just ironic—farcical. And yet she had decided she wanted marriage because she wanted children. 'We put on a white dress and then everyone imagine we are Virgin Marias, we lay our babies like eggs without sex.'

That night on the verandah, Pilar, laughing, looking into Bronagh's eyes, added, 'I decided I like to wear a black dress that day.'

Bronagh didn't react. She was remembering that time of walking around Cambridge with a heart so distended and stung that the slightest feeling was exaggeratedly painful and left her hollow, husked, chucked like an empty pistachio shell. Again and again she took herself to Monty's rooms where she sat by his gas fire. Usually he was moaning with boredom among his history books, 'Oh why can't I have been gifted for numbers like you, Bronagh? You mathematicians don't have to read and read.' Bronagh trusted Monty. He was the first person she had talked to about coming back with her mother to that low-skied northern town, their having to live on their guard against pity and worse, the commentary of those to whom her mother said a word or two outside mass and who thought she should be taken down a peg or two, reminded of the mistake she had made in marrying a man she imagined would turn her into Lady Muck. Monty always broke off willingly from his reading to talk to Bronagh. (Later, when he took a lower second-class degree—'more shameful than a third because it looks like you tried'—he would remind her half-bitterly how in those days he had never 'seen her crack open a book'.) Bronagh sat with her head turned gently sideways, listening. Monty never tried to stop her suffering. He said, 'It's because it's the first time, isn't it? The first time is always like this.' He told her a story of his own despair in a school library with the snow falling outside the window. Even now he couldn't bear to listen to the second movement of Bach's double violin concerto.

Bronagh knew Pilar was not virginal. There had been the very nice Italian on a motorbike who said, 'Are you still a virgin? You should get rid of it. Get it out of the way.' Of course she had seen Pilar too with her hair up on Saturday evenings, rimmelled and lipsticked with the matt red fruit stain that was the fashion this year everywhere, her Pilar turned into every other girl in the western world in the car of a friend on her way to dances in neighbouring villages. 'Come on, Bronagh, we are young. It's bad, dangerous to be too concentrated now.' So she had gone with them once or twice but soon got bored waiting for a lift back to San Gines. The excited, dialectal Spanish was beyond her, her head was too tight with gin and wine and anyway she didn't have the right clothes.

'How did you feel about it?' she had asked Pilar of the Italian. 'Did you regret it?'

'No.' Pilar said mildly. 'Because you can't know something until you experience it.'

Exactly. What had Pilar known? She always mentioned the

Italian with impersonal gratitude. Her heart had not been stung. Yet she spoke very explicitly about being a mother—unlike Bronagh she had been near to the process of gestation and childbirth, she had felt a fœtus kick at the walls of its mother's womb, something Bronagh had never even thought about. She talked with hushed sympathy of labours that went on for days because the baby had not turned round on its head as it should or had even died a day before birth, both of which refinements of nature had never crossed Bronagh's mind and still struck her, she who had never either suffered physically or witnessed physical suffering even in animals, as the sort of barbarism that belonged to another historical age.

Side by side on the verandah in that dusk, Pilar saw Bronagh's disquiet.

'Oh you are like the others!' she cried. 'You disapprove! Now I see women, men who take a political path, they are unhappy, and the same for a woman who behaves in a traditional way.' She laughed with her usual mockery but her eyes were wide, adamant, as when she thought she had come upon some limitation the person listening wished to impose upon her. 'Me, I use all my possibilities, as an old kind of woman, a new one … it depends but I choose. And this is a lot of fun!'

Bronagh remained more unmoved that evening than she would normally have been by the warmth of this speech. Perhaps it was her extreme physical tiredness or the cry that entered Pilar's voice when she said 'the others', or perhaps a return of that unreality she felt when Pilar recounted the details of childbirths in the village.

'It's all very well,' Bronagh said, leaning back reflectively with her drink. 'With children you won't be travelling or concentrating on anything else for a long time.'

'Why not? Why always one thing and then not another!' Pilar opened her hands. 'OK look I have just one. One child. Bronagh. I take him everywhere with me on my shoulders.'

'A boy?'

'Maybe! I want a girl. I won't think too much in case it's a boy and my thoughts hurt it. Oh, why not a boy? They are fun too.' She shrugged, placed her empty glass on the wooden railing and turned to Bronagh, eyes sparkling. 'So you don't think it's possible, Bronagh, to do all this?'

Bronagh sipped her drink although she knew she should stop drinking; the unreactive dough-like feel of that afternoon's useless sketching in the dry heat had come back in her, as if she were pressing her mind against some evidence from which no thought would take form.

'Why not? Everything's possible,' she said in tones that expressed the opposite. 'You have just one child, then you set it free.'

'Oh yes, you understand me, Bronagh. With just one we can do everything. I'll take it everywhere. We can go away.' She lifted her arm as though she was going to put it on Bronagh's shoulders, put her hard hand against the side of Bronagh's face, then inevitably with her forefinger stroked the place her hand had been. Bronagh didn't move. She didn't let any reaction show. Afterwards looking back she was sure of this, that her face had remained immobile. She had retreated into some crucial stillness as if in hiding from someone who must not by any sound or movement suspect she was there.

'I always thought I could love a face like this. Irish face sorry about the world.'

'No,' said Bronagh. She leaned carefully back from Pilar's hand. In the faded light her feet had taken on a whitish glow and ached to change position on the verandah railing, but any further movement would reveal too much. Pilar paused, then she too sat back away from Bronagh again. Mosquitoes and midges from the garden were making them uncomfortable. It was time to go inside but neither of them moved. *The bath*, Bronagh remembered. *I could say the generator's down.* But she determined to be as gentle and direct as possible. They were not going to lose their friendship over this. This mistake. A second later she knew she was wrong. Pilar, who had stayed uncharacteristically silent, said, 'So you are not a real artist. A real painter tries out everything, even just once. Maybe you love only numbers.'

Her usual mocking tone was there, even the peculiar warmth which was her gift when returning matters to their rightful size. But her face turned from Bronagh was unsmiling, her eyes lowered as if she were talking without hope to herself. She was humiliated, Bronagh saw. She herself could not think of what to say ... Better to wait patiently for the return of the language they shared so freely. But then Pilar lifted her face again and Bronagh was as startled as at the touch of the hand on the side of her face and as out of her depths again—*Oh no, not tears*—and also she was irritated because if Pilar was too blinded by her own feelings to try to understand Bronagh's then what was the point of talking?

'There were things you said,' Pilar said harshly. 'Other things you didn't.'

'What things?' said Bronagh.

'A friend of this Monty who is not your fiancé was here two years ago.'

'You never mentioned that you knew Monty before,' said Bronagh; her voice sounded shaken.

'They didn't like him in the village because of his clothes. Scarves with a French name on them.' Pilar stared sadly into the garden, pursuing her own train of thought rather than answering Bronagh, in a way that suggested her regal unconcern for Monty and his friends.

'And you are always against people not being able to dress how they like,' said Bronagh, but it was no use. That difficult quiet full of accusation had come back into the conversation, the silence that held when one person was full of important emotion and the other not at all. Pilar was chewing her nails, something Bronagh had never seen her do, then she stopped and stood up. From her friend's stance, her face discreet inside its hair curtain, she could tell the undone, humiliated expression was in her eyes again. Bronagh willed her to go, go on down the verandah steps before she started to cry and talk again. At the same time she recognized this lingering, this refusal to acknowledge finality. Of course she herself had played this scene before, in Pilar's role. Go on, go on, go! And Pilar was going, there in the unlit dark above the gleam of the road was the familiar sight of her back and her rapid walk, the leather belt on the neat waist above the torn-off trousers, the long, plainly-cut hair and the thin, strong calves, all these now more accessible to any other villager, to any other person in the world than to Bronagh for now all possibility had ended between them. She didn't look back, of course. Bronagh sat on feeling angry, accused, though not destroyed or even too wounded to think about sleep or using up the bathwater in the cistern for herself.

The morning dew had dried from the air next morning when

Bronagh walked down the chalk-coloured road into the village for bread long after her usual time. She hadn't slept well after all. The rusted gates, the house and the path up to the verandah looked as remote from her life, and at the same time as full of hidden meaning, as a house in a dream. She should have had a bath before going to bed the previous night but she had remained motionless for so long on the verandah that when she went inside she was aching all over with fatigue, yet whenever she closed her eyes that night her mind had focused powerfully on small images that convinced her she was still awake, still had the possibility of annulling that evening's mistake. She dreamt she was searching among the scrub grass and brown ants of the previous afternoon for her pencil. If she did not find it she would arrive back late at the villa and luckily miss Pilar waiting for her on the wooden verandah steps. The problem was she kept finding the pencil overrun by brown ants and thus kept arriving at Media Luna too soon, catching sight of Pilar waiting for her on the steps and then having surreptitiously to go all the way back into the scrub where she had been drawing in order to lose the pencil again. She woke late with a jolt, sweating already into steady sunlight. As if she were still dreaming, halfway down the chalk road this world of San Gines came simply and unquestionably to an end—hadn't she after all always half-known it would?—with the woman who worked in the village *correos* running up to meet her. She had a telegram in her hand and her hurry scattered the morning like a flock of startled birds.

Bronagh had never received a telegram before. She stood in the lane with the shiny sunlight all around her and wincing off the yellow paper of Telegrafica d'Espagna. Odd that she had forgotten that old childish nightmare, the news of her mother's death which would destroy the only child waiting in the dim flat and the cold, brackish smell off the Atlantic. Her mother was not dead. She was in hospital, not seriously ill but in considerable pain. They were going to operate on her back. The telegram came from a curate friend of hers, Fr Cassidy.

Bronagh turned and walked briskly back to the villa in the brightness of the early morning. Her hands were shaking. *Don't panic*, she told herself in a voice she didn't know she possessed, *keep to the facts*. Suprisingly, this meaningless injunction worked. She began to think calmly about how to go about getting away from San Gines. Even the young people rarely went into the bigger towns. Maybe she would have to spend several nights in a hotel in Granada waiting for the next train north. If so, how was she to book a hotel room, or arrange a taxi from San Gines to Granada? Without packing she left Media Luna and went down to the bakery to inquire about taxis to Granada. Her luck returned momentarily—a farmer had driven all the way out from Granada, over the potholed road in a rundown van, to sell the last of his winter vegetables. Bronagh could get a lift with him back into town. She walked back up to the villa again, her to-ing and fro-ing on the chalk road beginning to resemble the futilities of her dream. The verandah steps remained empty in the continuous sunlight. She wrote a postcard for Monty, packed her clothes and at the last minute, before locking up, left most of her sketchpads of ideas in a bin in the backyard. At the last minute, too, she poured about a third of a bottle of Ballantine's whisky into a silver flask that Monty had once given her as a joke. His own mother had made a gift of it to him on his departure for university, 'a man's thing and he was now a man'. It was pure silver, with on one side the etching of a naked woman with one slightly raised knee and arms lifted above her head of long hair. It might be useful to Bronagh on the train. She intended to keep afloat in a measured stupor from Granada to Paris, where she would have to sober up and start working out practical details again.

She closed all the shutters and set off. Cows grazed with particular motionlessness two fields away. The morning pasture-scented quiet remained unbroken as if no one had passed that way for days. The village walls gave off their usual ancient dusty, faintly cat-stinking smell in the hot sunshine, as they had every morning she had gone down to buy bread since she had arrived. Pilar was nowhere to be seen. The plaza was full of vegetable and fruit stalls on this market day. Her shoulders stiff and eyes evasive, Bronagh walked past the old black-clothed women watching her from the stalls. She had never been able to help imagining that these old women and the villagers in general disapproved of her, saw her as eccentric and depraved alone in the villa Media Luna, and for this reason she had difficulty in returning even the friendliest looks of interest from men or women in the streets or shops. In fact the village verdict was exactly that passed on her mother by those who had known her father out in Africa; they thought her secretive and old-fashioned and were disappointed by her understated clothes and plainly styled hair. The old women had noted the carefulness of her eyes and said 'Dry. Even for Inglesa.' Then in the plaza Pilar was hurrying towards her. With her rapid walk, slight form and dark hair she resembled many other young women of the village, and it was difficult in the dazzling morning light for Bronagh to distinguish a troubled note in her frank, dark eyes. She was smiling with her usual fresh health.

'You are leaving.'

Bronagh told her about the telegram. The expression in

Pilar's eyes did not change so it was hard to tell if she believed her or not. She gave back to Bronagh the yellowed paperback of *The Mill on the Floss*, which she had not finished but refused to keep, saying she would read it some other time.

'You didn't sleep well,' Pilar added rapidly, then smiled and went on, 'So maybe when you come back I'll be waiting for my child like a watermelon in the sun.' She laid her hand on her slim waist and for the last time gave Bronagh that challenging, self-mocking laugh. 'And you,' she said, 'an artist must draw every single day, work your hand, your eye.'

'Of course,' said Bronagh, foolishly. The reference touched off her self-pity—why had she not even once painted the hills, the white houses, the back of a chair, a bowl or towel in this light? Now she never would, for this return meant 'the painting' went back to its place in her mother's thoughts. A warm-weather pastime, a holiday hobby. 'Don't get angry and throw away bad drawings,' said Pilar. 'It doesn't matter, even if it's not good. Because of that bad drawing you do even better one tomorrow.' They put their arms around each other's shoulders and pulled towards each other in a careful upper-body hug, 'Look,' said Pilar, withdrawing, pointing in the direction of the drying sheepskins. Women were hurrying out to the farmer's van with messages and parcels to be left for relatives in the post office at Granada, and some of the old black-clothed women who sat against the wall in the market plaza were blessing themselves like a Greek chorus at the start of this journey all the way to the city.

Bronagh's journey north would take two days and a night, not counting the sitting through police checks, technical delays, re-routings and last-minute changes she had endured on the trip out and which Monty had warned her to expect when travelling by train. The seats and carpet of the first-class compartment smelt of warm dust; little powder bursts rose from the armrests and cushions when the passengers sat down. Opposite Bronagh a woman was arranging her luggage with the help of an officious older man and a youth who looked like their son. Yellowish lines stained the glass over the daguerreotypes of Madrid cafés above the velvet headrests. Bronagh felt the son's eyes taking her in curiously as she lifted her suitcase onto the rack. The older man saw her reaction and introduced himself and his wife and son. They exchanged a few polite sentences about their identity and their destination. The older man was a high-placed functionary in some ministry whose name Bronagh did not decipher. She herself explained she had been near Granada on holiday and the woman smiled approvingly. They were all going to San Sebastian, like Bronagh, to wait for the Paris train. Then the older man gave a small smile to belittle in advance any further comment. Their reserve would have pleased Bronagh's own mother, who called the curiosity of strangers 'a lack of finesse'. The woman opposite leaned forward to talk rapidly to her son and in a pleasant movement of colour and scent—unadulterated by the rank underlay of sweat—turned to her handbag, searched it, took out a box and pressed it without fuss into the youth's hand. Her hands were strong and elegant, the fingers ringed in gold and silver below the knuckle. Then the family settled and turned their eyes aside.

The train left Granada only fifteen minutes late. Bronagh's *Herald Tribune*, bought to deter conversation—'West Berlin Must Not Be Given to the Communists'—dropped onto her knees; at that time of her life she never read newspapers anyway. She did not know enough to read between the lines and the fascination with communism bored her because she had never in her life been seriously afraid as the newspapers told her she should be.

The train slipped out through the poor gypsy ghettoes of the Granadan suburbs. Bronagh had closed her eyes. She was on her way home. She felt again the initial disarray of that child alone in the dark house, the forgotten but familiar sound of her mother's name overheard in childhood in her father's mouth, the soft, over-ironed feel of a dark-green linen blouse her mother wore as she hugged her when she came back to the flat on the harbour at Portdoran at the end of the term, her mother's dry, repetitive cough that was not even like a cough but the syllable of a throat cleared nervously over and over as if to force a sentence out.

Sevilla, Toledo, Madrid, San Sebastian, France. She could trace out the route on the map under yellowed glass above the black-haired head of the youth opposite. Already just over three hours out of Granada the air filtering through the window had lost that swooning evening smell of burnt earth and plant transpiration and taken on a fresher, sharper scent. Then through the stained window the late afternoon sunlight was the colour of nicotine on the orange and white houses of villages and towns. The son seated opposite wore black leather boots, the laces tied intricately around a row of steel knobs. Bronagh glanced up and flinched from the direct gaze of black eyes under heavy eyebrows and a long face whose dark bad temper resembled the tightly knotted boots. There was something wrong with him, how had she not seen it until now? She looked away at once, though careful not to do so too quickly.

'*Dame, dame eso,*' said the woman to her son, holding out her hand impatiently, a gesture incongruent with the strong, long hand and its rings, which like the rich clothes she wore denoted social weight. '*Lo que tienes en la mano! Lo que has escondido!*' Glancing up at Bronagh, the woman lowered her voice. The old man went on intently in his book. The afflicted youth sat hunched in his seat, black hair drooping over either side of his face, until the mother shook her outheld hand and then he began taking something out of his pocket. Bronagh felt eyes rising towards her and again she looked for a long moment out of the window, after which the woman had settled back into her seat, and the son sat with bowed head, glowering at a handkerchief balled in his hand. The woman had seen her watching. She told Bronagh matter-of-factly, speaking English, 'When our son was three years he had meningite. We were posted in the south, a little town in the Sierra Morena. We did not go to the big hospital in the city. We did not have good doctors and now our son is like this.'

'I'm sorry,' said Bronagh. She was shocked and then afraid her shock would sound offensive.

The other woman's head went back in a gesture that meant she didn't care what Bronagh felt now that she had explained what was wrong with her son. She said nothing more. The man with his eyes closed beside her didn't move to comment on the accusation, if that was what it was, in this short account. Maybe neither of them heard any accusation in the words.

At Toledo the train sat in its own heat and dust for well over an hour. Bronagh got out and sat dazed in a *comedor* behind the station bar, nauseated by the uncustomary stillness in the floor at her feet and, when she ordered a *café cortado*, by the smell of the milk they heated to a froth before they put it in the coffee. In this crowd, where she could sit for the first time in months without being seen, she was not relaxed. Newspaper stands sported the usual headlines in Spanish, French and English. Megaton Nuclear Explosion Planned for Oct 30. Government Exhorts West to Resist Atomic Blackmail. For the first time since she had come to Spain the old uncertainty she had felt after university about the part she wanted to play in this world returned in force. A group of Americans younger than Bronagh sat outside the *comedor*, dressed in gypsy scarves and playing songs on their guitars while they waited for their train. The station security guards arrived and moved them on, told them to stop playing music and to sit on the benches provided. Later in Bronagh's life, when she had lived as much again, she never knew what to say when young people asked her what was it like to live at this time, so near, they implied, to the beginning of the time when 'young people' saw themselves as such and made their 'revolution' against the world. I am not the one to ask, she would have liked to say. I was there but I wasn't picked up by the current. At least not in the way you like to imagine. It was almost impossible later to conjure up her apartness at that time, to understand if it had to do with her detachment from a prevailing religious attitude to peace, to communism, the end of the world, or simply characterized her own dormant state of waiting and seeking for a point at which to begin carrying out her destiny.

She was not the only foreigner now among the Spanish townspeople and country travellers drinking the confusingly multi-named variety of Andalucian sherries with their *tapa*. There were other foreigners, Germans, French and an English family talking loudly over their luggage as if convinced the sound of their language entertained everyone. She had got out of the habit of understanding the words of strangers on first hearing. Also, these northerners appeared so pallid, skinless almost; surely they were not her compatriots. The sun had changed her; her skin was of that northern type which the sun turns healthy light gold, more Scandinavian than Irish.

They had come through Toledo. Her head had cleared. A journey this long was like toothache, pain between periods of energetic lucidity. After nightfall someone opened the compartment window, letting in fresh air smelling of earthy countryside. Bronagh felt an uprush of confidence and well-being like the false joy that possesses one in convalescence. Every detail of the compartment, with its worn seats and brownish wallpaper, seemed portentous. She studied the family opposite with great interest, overcoming her usual timorousness at looking strangers in the eyes. Between waking and dozing off with the unread *Herald Tribune* on her knees, she imagined she had told them everything and they had already talked together with real warmth and sympathy and exchanged invitations to their homes in Madrid and Ireland, but then each time she woke up properly it was to look into the old man's head bowed over his book. He had changed places with his wife at Toledo, when the Guardia Civile had run quickly through the train checking passports and luggage. Now he sat opposite Bronagh, still reading his small, thick book. The same grave expression remained on his small, downturned mouth. At his side his wife appeared much younger than you would think if you saw her alone in her expensive clothes with her haughty gaze out the window. Only the son acknowledged Bronagh's presence as he slouched in his corner, staring arrogantly at her in his tight jacket buttoned up to his neck like some brace accentuating the heavy discontent of his body. By contrast, the father's concentration, when one looked carefully, exuded the energy of a muscular and skilled acrobat. The clothes, too, a waistcoat finely woven from a thin cloth of dark yellow thread, with the tiny, black insignia of an Italian *maison de couture* figured on one of the lapels, denoted the care and precision implicit in this stillness. This touch of the dandy, the impregnable self-confidence of that finely spun material, amazed Bronagh. Immediately, with the fastidiousness of which Pilar's mockery had not totally cured her, she passed judgement on him. 'There', she thought, 'is the power that holds these two with him.' For a minute she even despised the mother and son. She felt she knew all about them, particularly the woman, and their connection with that dry, powerful old man. Who could kiss that mouth with love?

Bronagh began drinking in snatches from the silver flask, aware at first but then not caring how it made her look. In her stomach the whisky made a bitter pool and would not pass into her bloodstream. The memory of her mother's dislike of alcohol came back to her—the look on her face that only Bronagh could see when she smelt it on others and also the mild confusion of anger and pity the image awoke in her. Bronagh's destination, that coastline with the light sometimes shining through the chapel windows of the grey convent school on the promontory, where the air was as wild as around some lonely outpost farm in the African veldt, now felt as insubstantial as those shuttered afternoons she had left behind. She could not believe that more real than Pilar or the routine of her days in

Media Luna would be that wet wind that flaked the cream paint on the outside walls and left its salt smell even in the permanent dusk of the stairwell where the people in the first-floor flat piled her mother's mail on a curly ormolu side table. When they first came back from Africa, the summers were so cold, the sky so low and flattening, that even her mother, who had grown up in Portdoran, complained and shivered through July and August. In Bronagh's bedroom in the flat on the harbour, there was a doll's house and a rocking horse with gorgeous chocolate eyes.

Dustmotes turned in the yellow light. In her pockets Bronagh's fingers touched pieces of torn paper. She pulled them out and saw the crumpled pieces of telegram which she thought she had thrown away in the bin at the back of Media Luna. The paper was damp from the sweat of her clenched hand as she slept. Now the train raced through a blue-lidded, shiny-leaved spring afternoon. Bronagh had eaten little—nothing—the previous day. Her appetite had gone. Opposite her the mother worked tirelessly to keep her son comfortable and quiet, feeding him, taking him out of the carriage to the toilets, standing with him in the corridor where he pressed his face to the breeze of the window aperture, and in the compartment talking ceaselessly in low, insistent tones to him when boredom made him scratchy and ill at ease. The youth listened to her, his face turned away from the words, his thin, black hair askew on his face. 'The deformed child to which Europe had given birth,' thought Bronagh. The words were from a sentence overheard on the radio of the café back at San Gines—part of the usual rant against communism, but its hate had shocked her even through the haze of a language imperfectly understood: 'This deformed child shall be extirpated in the flesh from the streets and families of the villages and towns.' When Bronagh concentrated, the gentle voice of the mother was always talking about nice, pretty things to look at and eat. *'Pájaros de colores cantarines que se venden en jaulas de acedera.'* Pretty coloured birds in wicker cages. *'Vamos a beber chocolate juntos temprano por la mañana cuando todos los demas estén durmiendo.'* We'll go and drink chocolate in the warm morning when everyone else is asleep. The train passed countless simple round-roofed churches, domed like the mosques of the Arab invaders nearly a thousand years ago. Pilar would marry, and divorce would be impossible in Catholic, Franquist Spain. Bronagh opposed marriage because she had never understood why her parents had married, why, having separated from her husband, her mother should listen to the priests arguing that 'those whose faith gave them the courage for a bad marriage' must be happier than 'those unknowingly trapped by lust or material greed'. She would not be convinced by Bronagh's encouraging her to imagine a new life in a different country. Spain, for instance. A Roman Catholic country her mother would feel at home in, far from their pariah-like existences in Portdoran where the parish priests were her mother's only friends. After her father's death, Bronagh had attempted to persuade her mother to sell off the flat. She had even drawn up an estate agent's description and showed it to her.

'We can go anywhere now. The south of France, Italy. I'll arrange everything.'

Bronagh took a while to grasp that her mother was as married in death as in life, also that though bullied from the beginning, she had always found her own way out, as quietly as water finds out a chink. Her mother had stopped the sale of the flat not by imposing herself directly but with faint smiles, with tiredness and looking away.

Every three or four hours, the young man started moaning '*Qué vamos a hacer?*' and the woman looked at a watch she took from her handbag, then from under the seat pulled a food hamper to serve her husband and child.

'*Qué me das ahí?*' said the father. Without lifting his eyes from his book he took from her the napkin-wrapped roll and bit into it. The son stopped complaining, then snatched the sandwich and ate in silence, holding out a small cup to fill with flat-smelling red wine. The *bocadillos* contained *paté del país*, and the sweaty, intimate smell of their eating and drinking soon filled the warm air of the compartment. Once, for politeness' sake, they offered Bronagh some food, and politely she refused. She had bought a tortilla, which proved too oily to ingest, along with a mineral water. The old man uncrossed and crossed his legs and continued reading, his mouth set implacably as ever against conversation. After an eating session his wife arranged the hamper and rested her ornate head on the dusty velvet, like the head of a queen on a coin. On her face in repose could be read the trace of time and toil, probably the work of caring for the sick son not visible in her waking, thinking face. Unhealthy brown shadows under her eyes contrasted the artistry of the strong, sculpted face, the pride of her jewellery and clothes. Side by side with the old man bent over his book, she closed her eyes. Her son stayed awake but remained still, a napkin from his lunch balled in his hand, gazing with his flushed face and his perpetual anger out of the window, as if the train were taking him further and further from where he wanted to be.

Night had come over Spain several hours ago. The air in the compartment was cooler. The elder functionary had closed his book and gone out to smoke in the corridor, leaving his son sulky-faced in sleep with his head on his mother's knee. For an hour the train had been pulling into some town Bronagh couldn't identify from the map framed on the wall opposite. Finally they came to rest in the dingiest, smokiest railway station Bronagh had ever seen. In the distance, metal clanged, voices floated into high, stained rafters, passengers hurried up and down the aisle outside their compartment. Dazed they sat on together in the new silence that had replaced the noise of the wheels on the rails, then they heard people calling the name of the town to each other. Burgos. The old man came back into the compartment and looked as if he might say something important, but he sat down without speaking. Footsteps resounded through the corridor outside. From called-out conversations came the news of strikes, unrest at Barcelona and Bilbao. Bronagh thought briefly of the violence in the stories she had heard in San Gines, the bodies tossed into ravines, the arrests and disappearances, but the stories had been everywhere so long she wasn't afraid. The woman bent her head and began to talk gently to her restless son, '*para una noche, cariño sola una noche*'. She caught Bronagh's eye briefly and for the first time sent her the most fleeting of sympathetic smiles, then she looked away.

The train sat on. There was no point in going out, for all the bars and station cafeterias and *comedors* had closed for the night. While the lights stayed on they could not go to sleep properly. They were all waiting to see if someone would push open the door of the compartment and take over the space they had got used to after occupying it alone together for the best part of nearly two days. The son awoke and sat up and the mother lifted down the food basket and gave him bread and *ensaladilla*, then looked out the window without interest as he ate. When at long last the train moved off again they had given up hope and were half dozing dry-eyed in the bright electric light. Bronagh was fed up. She unscrewed the flask and poured drink into herself, tipping her head back quickly as if she were taking medicine.

Daybreak was still hours away. They were heading for the border at San Sebastian, then she would get out and wait for the French train to Paris. The daguerreotype map showed Irun as the last Basque town near the French border but it seemed that they would never get out of Spain. Time, all motion, were now fixated on the need to arrive. Outside the black windows Bronagh envisaged the Basque country, which in San Gines they said was ugly, with bad roads and dark, industrialized towns. That information from villagers who had never been as far north as Madrid, along with folk wisdom that the Basques had enormous appetites and disliked work, was the sum total of Bronagh's knowledge of this part of the Iberian peninsula. Stark, undercultivated plains, they had told her. Arid, empty after our green Andaluz hills with their white walls round castle and church. But the hours of the journey had worn down Bronagh's initial nostalgia for the sunlight and the heat, the bread, the pool in the rocks, the wine in the plaza. Pilar. All that satiation of the south. Soon she would be in France. France, with bluish, greenish lavender tints in its deepest south, was the start of the North.

bronagh

The electric lights in the compartment fizzed, then stayed off. Bronagh slept lightly, woke when the lights flickered on again, saw in her reflection in the dark window her hand limply over the silver flask, noted how her long body, the set of her fair-haired head, resembled her father's. The boy was awake. She couldn't see his face in the dark where his parents slept seated upright, heads side by side on the velvet headrests like sculpted figures on a tomb. She remembered his mother taking off his boots so he could sleep comfortably on the seat. Bronagh waited without moving, then shifted her head slightly and closed her eyes as if she were sleeping; could he have made out her open eyes in the dark? She sat back, gave up the pretence of sleeping then looked up, shocked by the energy and anger in the eyes under the heavy eyebrows.

'*Perdoneme*,' she said softly. She glanced at his sleeping parents as if to enjoin him to be reasonable and not wake them up. But at her voice he made a sound that alarmed her, pulled back with a grimace. Bronagh thought he was in pain.

'*Señor? Lo siento?*'

Outside fields and houses passed in thick blue shadow under the moonlight. When she thought he had relaxed she glanced up covertly, only to hear him make a tight noise as if in that dim light her regard was unbearable for him.

This time she awoke abruptly in the embarrassed certainty that she had been snoring. The electric lights had come on full. The other woman was looking at her for the first time, as if she had just broken off some comment. They stared at each other for a moment, her handsome eyes were dark like a horse's. Something in her expression made Bronagh think she was waiting for her to speak. The son's boots had been ranged side by side under the seat; he had curled up, as much as it was possible for a youth of his size to curl up, his legs bent at the knees, and he slept at last, silently, his mouth open. They had closed the window tightly so that, she supposed, he would sleep like a child in the heat. The air in the compartment smelt nauseously of sweat and unwashed clothes. The old man had folded his pince-nez and closed his book, he had pulled back the pleated leather curtain over the glass separating them from the corridor that ran along First Class. His eyes without his glasses looked bigger and round.

'*Perdoneme, donde estamos?*' Bronagh asked. Using words was like continuing in another language the conversation of the past two days. The old man remained immobile as if she hadn't spoken, the back of his neck turned to look under the small leather curtain.

'*No se,*' said the woman. She shrugged. 'San Sebastian. Basque country.'

The woman turned, following her husband's regard out of the compartment window into the dim corridor. The night behind the window at Bronagh's side of the compartment reflected the sleeping youth's large, unrelaxed face and nothing of the outside world. From the surrounding quiet she could tell they had stopped in the middle of the country. She was about to ask what was happening when the old man leaned forward and switched off the compartment light. His wife said nothing, the son continued to sleep. Almost as if she had laid her hand on the old man's shoulders, Bronagh could feel the tension in his back and neck attentive at the compartment window. She didn't know what to make of the complicated and ominous atmosphere that had suddenly entered the compartment. On the other side of the corridor revealed by the lifted curtain, the train window gave onto still blackness where insects flitted in the crude light of big electric lamps shining on a new concrete platform. Basque country was bandit country. Details from government posters and radio propaganda now came back to her. Her first thought was that the government official must fear for his own well-being, and indeed the woman's face was stony now, concentrated like her husband's on the blank scene revealed through the lifted curtain. Bronagh opened her mouth to speak; she must even have said something for without looking back at her, the old man held up a hand for silence and then they heard the sound of feet hurrying along the corridor.

Everything happened very quickly.

The door of the compartment opened and the light was snapped on. Two small unshaven men in khaki with guns over their shoulders stood in the doorway, flanking a taller, cleaner man, unarmed and wearing a long, grey scarf around his neck.

'*Control de identificación!*' said one of the soldiers.

The woman opened her bag and held out folded cards which were taken, flicked open and passed to the officer in the doorway. Moans of pain and surprise came from the seat opposite; the young man was waking up and complaining about his boots—'*En donde has puesto mis botas? Quién ha cogido mis botas?*' —and his mother was talking again to quieten him. '*No hables, por favor, ahora, no.*'

'*Quién es ese?*'

The man in the doorway indicated Bronagh to the old man, who opened his hands philosophically.

'*Aquí está mi pasaporte,*' said Bronagh, handing it to the first soldier. It was an Irish passport.

'*De donde vienes?*'

'*De Irlanda.*'

The soldier broke in, '*No, no. Donde has cogido el tren?*'

'*Ah, perdone, señor,*' said Bronagh. Appallingly she did not have the reflex to let go of that inappropriate confidence that was Pilar's rather than her own, though she understood this tone was reckless and thought she saw the woman opposite look at her husband.

'*La pregunta no estaba clara para mi. Soy inglesa, pero he cogido el tren en Granada.*'

The grey-scarved man at the door turned away.

'*Ven, ven, vamos a ver eso,*' said the first soldier, taking Bronagh's arm, and when Bronagh in a sudden rush of humiliation resisted, the second soldier grabbed her other arm roughly, igniting a flare of hatred she had never felt before. She looked into hazel eyes in a dark face with as much violence as she was capable of before the soldier turned her round and pushed her out of the compartment. '*Ya has oido*, We see paper, OK? OK?' and as they went out the old man withdrew his feet neatly to let them past. This little gesture, more than the soldiers' rough hands, made Bronagh frightened at last at having slipped so rapidly outside the pale of ordinary safety. She stumbled as the door of the compartment was pushed closed behind them.

The air in the corridor was refreshingly chill. Her legs ached from prolonged sitting and from the weakness of not having eaten well for so long. From the other passenger compartments came a nightmarish stillness. No one else had been hauled out for this extra paper and identity check. What had happened to all the over-loud, pale-kneed Brits and Germans, her people, defenceless unaesthetic northerners she had watched with mild condescension hauling their luggage and signalling to each other in the station bars of Toledo and Madrid? The soldiers with guns pushed Bronagh down to a space between the toilets and a train door she had last climbed down from, yawning and stiff, to force herself to buy food at a station stall.

The taller man in the grey scarf was waiting.

'You have problem. *No visado de salida*. No exit visa.' He flapped the passport in the air as if the pages were blank.

'*Qué visado de salida?*' Bronagh asked. The other man said with the same soft accent, '*Estas putas inglesas de mierda.*'

Bronagh had come sufficiently to her senses to resist that wild anger which had threatened to make her lose herself in the compartment. She let the hazel-eyed soldier reach into her pockets and take out the silver flask that had belonged to Monty's mother's father. Act naïve, she told herself. She waved her hands to convey her harmlessness and summon the language to convince these men that they had made a mistake, she did not understand what an exit visa was.

'*No necesito visado de salida! Tengo pasaporte!*'

The tall man closed her passport and placed it in his pocket.

'New rules,' he said in English.

He looked out quickly, as if checking for activity under the white electric light. 'It is late.' He added, '*Démonos prisa. El tren sale dentro de dos minutos.*'

'But I have to get to Paris. Le Havre. For the boat to Ireland,' said Bronagh, dropping Spanish in a sort of plea for his comprehension as an English-speaker. 'I have to go home to Ireland.' English sounded both weak and arrogant, dangerously so. For an answer she had the hard eye of a rifle in her back for the first time in her life. The tall man had turned his back on her, the soldiers were pushing her out of the train, which would go on without her. She remembered talk in San Gines about borrowing women's scarves to go to market in, so that if attacked by brigands the villagers could cover their faces and stand a greater chance of escaping with their lives. The metal was hard against her back again, but then new movement was taking place in the corridor behind them.

'Don't move or say anything,' said a voice confidentially in English. A hand was laid on her arm, the rifle butt moved from her back. Bronagh turned to see the calm, withered face of the old man, big-eyed without his pince-nez. He said, *'Esta persona, esta como se dice, bajo mi protección.'*

The tall man had turned back, his pale face over the scarf registered no surprise.

'No comprendo,' he said, formal and in control like a sarcastic schoolteacher. Without smiling, he opened his hands in imitation of the gesture the old man had made disowning Bronagh in the compartment. *'Además no tiene visado de salida.'*

Bronagh felt the old man's dry hand pat her back. *'Viajamos juntos.'* His steady hand came down on Bronagh's arm again and this time it tightened to underline its possession. *'Visado de salida, visado de salida, va a terminar enfadándome!'* he said with force. These things can be sorted out.

To Bronagh he pointed in the direction of the compartment where yellow light shone into the corridor. 'Go on back there now.'

The two soldiers stood back. Bronagh walked away, trying not to scurry. She pushed back the compartment door. As soon as she met the woman's regard the dark eyes changed with relief as if a question had been answered.

'Venga siéntese, come in, quick, sit down,' she said.

'*Gracias*,' said Bronagh. She was shaking. After the fresh night air outside in the corridor, the overheated body smells in the compartment made her stomach rise. The young man was sleeping again deeply, his hair over his flushed face damp with the excess of that sleep.

'For hours he sleeps this way,' said the woman, naturally, as if they had been chatting like this throughout the journey from Granada. She was talking to reassure Bronagh, to calm her down. Her English, unlike her husband's, was slow and accented.

'Is the … *medicinas* …'

'Medication.'

'Yes.'

Bronagh ran her hand over her face because the woman's kindness made her want to let go of her self-control and weep noisily like a child. She lowered her hand to contain the trembling.

'Look, what's happening out there, do you know?' she asked.

The woman gave the same fatalistic shrug Bronagh had seen in the village. It didn't mean that they didn't know or care but that they were the butt of some situation not worth wasting time attempting to understand. Eventually the other woman said, 'They talk.' As if making small talk she added, 'His English is perfect. Not like my English.' She arranged her son's coat, which had slipped off his sleeping shoulders. Her face in its heavy, sculpted beauty above her son was composed and as unpreoccupied as when Bronagh had watched her sleep with her head poised against the headrests. Gently the woman pushed strands of black hair back from her son's wet forehead.

'It's good when he sleeps. It makes him well,' she murmured. The expression of the youth's face red in sleep, his open mouth, struck Bronagh as leering, even self-satisfied, and the woman's caress pathetically incongruent with the damp, sweaty ugliness of its object. She sighed with fear and tension, clasped her hands to stop them shaking and looked out at the blank reflecting dark of the train window which returned their images like a mirror.

'*No se preocupe.* Don't worry,' said the woman kindly to her. The rough smell of black-tobacco cigarettes came through the closed door. The kindness of the woman's words made her miss Pilar and then she remembered that the old, complicit Pilar was lost anyway forever.

'Bandit country. But they're not Basques, they're not speaking Euskadi,' Bronagh said abruptly.

'Euskera,' said the other woman. 'Euskadi the country. Euskera the language. *Ya salió, no se trataba de vascos.*' She repeated slowly in English. 'No, they are not Basques, Guardia Civile.'

Bronagh stared at her but decisive movement in the corridor left no time for questions. She held her breath, her heart hammered with fear at the memory of the rifle butt in her back. She would have liked to squeeze her eyes shut or jump up, open the door and start pleading with them to argue her case. It was an effort of will to remain seated and waiting where she was in the pure fear that now obliterated all trace of that earlier heedless anger. Voices rose but not violently, followed by clatter and shouts outside in the night air. She cleared her throat.

'*El tren tiene que salir.*' Her Spanish sounded ridiculously prudent, anglicized. 'One of them said we would have to be off in a few minutes.'

If they were Guardia Civile then they were not communists, nor anarchists like Pilar's brother. She thought incon-
gruously of a witticism that a priest friend of her mother's who
used to come to their house was fond of repeating about the
communists. 'They're wrong, sure it's God not the capitalists
who distributes suffering in this world.' She was empty,
aching, she could not make herself concentrate on some mental trick to get the time by. She had never considered herself
capable of hysteria but one minute more and her mind would
no longer respond to this injunction to stillness. If only the
train would start now and the functionary come back and the
lights to go out so that they could all go to sleep again and she
would be saved. But they might wait for several hours despite
the words of the man in the grey scarf on the necessity of leaving at once; at this her despair was so total she could hardly
raise her eyes to the woman opposite, who was smoothing her
son's hair lightly, to comfort or keep him asleep in the intense
heat of the motionless train. He turned on his back, his face up
to the light, but continued sleeping profoundly, open-
mouthed, outstretched on the seat, head pushed, like an
infant's in the womb, against his mother's body. Bronagh
leaned back opposite the stained daguerreotypes of Madrid,
then the floor shifted beneath their feet, the lights buzzed and
the train was pulling out into the night again. She was safe.
But still she sat rigidly as the fear ebbed from her body, as if
the slightest change of position had the power to upset whatever balance of forces had saved her.

The old man entered the compartment, shutting the door
carefully behind him as if they might have fallen asleep in his
absence.

'So. All's well that ends well. Your passport is "lost",' he said with satisfaction, indicating the inverted commas with a gesture of the hands. 'When we stop at San Sebastian, you get over to the border police and report it stolen. They should give you a *laissez-passer* into France.'

'Yes. Thank you,' said Bronagh.

'By and large you got off lightly, wouldn't you say?' he said cheerfully; perhaps he had noticed the strain on her face and was trying to cheer her up.

But I didn't do anything wrong, she thought fractiously; she didn't dare to say anything now that the fear was leaving her, and she felt humiliated at finding herself like the child she had been, too afraid to dare expressing anger.

He nodded, ignoring her, and arranged himself on the seat. Maybe only his wife could read the deep hard lines at the corners of the mouth and between the pale eyebrows. The youth had begun breathing loudly with a small snore at the end of each breath ...

'*En este asunto, tiene que darle las gracias a mi mujer.*'

You have my wife to thank for my intervention. This switch back to Spanish along with the dimming of the lights signalled official discontinuation of interest in the matter. Then he sat back and closed his big eyes.

A little while later Bronagh saw the woman raise her face to her in the dark.

'I saw you this evening. When my son could not sleep. You were kind to him.' The woman left a small pause then, but went on almost at once. 'We are tired,' she said, including Bronagh in the sentence. 'You should sleep now also.'

After that the woman slept silently, head straight against the seat. Bronagh closed her eyes but her brain was racing. One moment she believed she understood the past and its connection to the future as never before; the next moment she felt jabbing panic at this train taking her nearer and nearer to where she didn't want to be and at the idea of explaining her story at San Sebastian, then facing the family waiting for her in the town where she had grown up. At last sleep came. But all that had nearly happened returned her to an exhaustingly sad dream in which she went on a journey with a child who in the course of that journey somehow got lost. She searched for the child with increasing desperation, then she was awake, gasping in the thick dark of the train compartment at night, still in the clothes she had put on in Media Luna nearly two days ago now. Opposite was the form of the youth stretched out in heavy sleep, his head on his mother's knees.

The train had swung through the last towns of the Spanish Basque country before France. Cold air filtered into the carriage. From early morning the lights came on properly again and the window still dark and noisy with wind and rails reflected the fine, small ankles of the old man crossed as he slept and his feet shod in close-fitting, almost dainty shoes. The woman still slept fitfully, motionless against the seat. The early morning smelt of cinder.

When Bronagh arrived in Portdoran her mother had been transferred from hospital to a long-stay nursing home overlooking the grey and brown vaults and billows of her beloved Atlantic. The arrangements had already been carried out by her mother's friend Fr Cassidy. Most of all Bronagh had been dreading the flat where she had spent her childhood; she had even decided to pay for a hotel, or a room in one of the bed-and-breakfasts along the promenade of short, undecorated grey and white houses, rather than sleep in those rooms again. But when she went to the flat on the harbour, the past had gone. The bell jar beneath which life in those rooms had withered like a forgotten bouquet had lifted forever. The doors of her parents' bedroom stood wide, the dull March light spread over bookshelves and the bottle-green carpet of her girlhood with an unexpected air of completeness like a stage set after the last show. The great double bed ridiculously outsized for the room it dwarfed, the bed in which Bronagh had been conceived and born, with its grave, overwrought headboard and pillows of Irish linen, had turned into a monument that would probably outlive Bronagh too.

When Bronagh was fourteen she went away from Portdoran. Her father would not hear of her receiving a Roman Catholic education so she did not go to the convent on the promontory but to boarding school in Malvern, England. There she found friends who were from different countries and whose parents sometimes lived apart. She was gaining access to that section of society in which she would by her late teens have visited important galleries in Europe, learned a modern language, and published Latin doggerel in the school magazine. Without any doubt she preferred school-life to that in the flat on the Atlantic shore where her father came and went more often now in her absence. At Easter of the year he died she arrived home two days after he left for Kenya for the last time. When he died there was not enough money to repatriate the body and Bronagh's mother travelled alone to Nairobi for the burial.

Perhaps because Bronagh did not attend the funeral, the question of John Wycherley, of an old ambition to find evidence to make her mother hate him and leave him for good, remained unresolved. By the time of his death she had not so much given up as forgotten to search any more for proof against the enemy, but then his death had removed him into the baffling and total silence that presses down from the universe where there is pain.

A few years after his death Bronagh read a study detailing the life of the White Highlanders, the vanishing class for which her father had worked on the farm in Kenya. There, after pages on farming problems, rinderpest, sheep-pox and the local Masai, the author quoted an extract from a ledger dated the year of her birth, 1942:

Picnic, June 2.
Gin (Beefeater's, three cases)
Whisky (10 Bottles)
Champagne (Sixteen Magnum)
40 bot. Fresh root beer.
6 bot. tawny port.
10 bot. light rum
Wine: 10 sweet rosé, French Red, Portuguese White.

Ishmael fined three shillings and horsewhipped for rubbing silver plate on the grass to clean it and this after several previous warnings. Morning's hunt, glorious grass, no holes. Ten couple of hounds, all the Seguin strain.

In her mind's eye Bronagh kept seeing her father's name after the word 'horsewhipped', with its horrible sound of tearing leather. She should have known better than to take the book to her mother, who laid the novel she was reading on her neat knee and read the page Bronagh showed her, peering slightly as if it were another language, then handed it back with an odd little disgusted movement of the shoulder. 'All that drink! How they drink, you can't imagine.' She looked into her daughter's face. 'You left Africa when you were little more than a baby,' she said. 'Twenty years, a lifetime he was out there, poor man.' It took Bronagh a minute to understand these last words meant her father. 'They say your father understood them better than they did themselves.'

On the streets people took in her tanned face, the sunlit blue of her eyes. They were saying she was the spit of John Wycherley. She allowed herself to feel a superior sense of unbelonging, much as her father must have done among the dour-faced houses set to the Atlantic, the sunless skies, the frumpy, pale faces. No one expected her to stay much longer in Portdoran. Two red-haired cousins on her mother's side had turned up from London. They urged her to come back with them to their flat in south London where they had a sofa-bed in a spare room. 'Sure most nights one or other of us is not there any more.' She left her mother to the vigil over her father's spirit begun many years before his death, and went with them to London. They were full of admiration, these girls her new-found cousins, for the different life they had found over the water, for cars and rock 'n' roll and anonymity. One of them was engaged to a building contractor, the other going steady with a teacher. They were well-built, pale-faced women dressed in the miniskirts of the dance-floors. They thought they were living a remake of the swinging twenties. In the next five years they would have two children each; they had no anger as yet, no sense of the banality stalking them.

They looked after her with real kindness, making her

meals, taking her out to drink with them (though she was drinking less and less), 'pulling her leg' by joking about things she only half listened to. Bronagh told Monty how they called her 'the unknown quantity'. She didn't see Monty often, however; he was never alone now that he had set up in Knightsbridge and she no longer felt free to drop in on him. Thus she never got round to talking to him as she had planned about the intense fear she had experienced on the train or how it had struck her that a need similar to the desire she now felt for camouflage might explain the curiously cumbersome and valuable furniture with which he had filled his flat. The cousins were trying to persuade her that her best bet was to emigrate. 'Not that one place is that different from another, sure the same bunch of crooks is in the top jobs everywhere. Take your time, Bronagh. Travel around for a while,' they said.

However, after Spain Bronagh's tactics had changed. The uncertainty remained but she shied away from travel now, wanting the relief of belonging to a crowd. The journey home had wearied her as if it had required some unrelenting watchfulness and concentration. She did not think that this tiredness would ever fade; she concluded that most people were meant to stay in one place where their faces and habits grew familiar to those around them, and she concluded that she was like most people. She wanted her days filled up with ordinary activity.

She obtained a post to teach maths in a private Catholic girls' school near London. She imagined it was a bit like it might have been teaching in the convent on the Atlantic promontory where John Wycherley would not have heard of her receiving an education. She worked there for three years, living in the spare room on the cousins' sofa-bed when one of the cousins, married now with a pre-school daughter, went through a bad phase, stopped going out around London and stayed at home on Valium. Bronagh had to look after the child. She enjoyed drawing the little girl over to her. She was moved by the purity of her world where nothing was yet decided, and also by the contradiction that in spite of all she herself knew, she was not going to teach the child that this was the worst of all worlds and that nobody had understood it yet. Instead she loved the power of giving her the names of objects and their uses, the difference between what really was and what seemed to be. When the cousin recovered and threw the Valium packs and prescriptions into the duck-pond of one of the London parks, Bronagh resigned her teaching post and went out to Kenya to a job as a research assistant in the faculty of maths and physics in Nairobi. Her mother's health in the Portdoran nursing home had stabilized enough for her to travel far away again. Academically speaking the Nairobi position was a dead end, but the fear she had known after Spain was gone, displaced by curiosity about this country her mother had arrived in as her father's bride. In Kenya she met a scientist opposed to mechanistic atheism, a biologist researching DNA structure for whom the double helix, the spirals of DNA, were intertwined in a loving embrace. A man who threw himself into her quiet, arguing himself drunk on assertions of self-transforming faith in the existence of God. She married him because of how he laughed half-passionately at the spectacle of his despair over her—'Your blindly indifferent universe is a piece of wishful thinking! We all want to be free of moral constraints!'—and not for his propounding the designs of wasp-imitating orchids and dancing bees.

Bronagh thought about Pilar a lot in the period when she was pregnant with their first child. She had become effortlessly happy again, as in the summer she had spent in San Gines when she was twenty-three. She stopped working in the faculty at Nairobi and painted with more courage than she had managed before. One painting was of a pregnant woman, recognizable from the pinkness of her feet as Pilar from San Gines after the hot baths she loved. She was standing, looking out of an upstairs window into a garden where night was drawing in. There was no recrimination in her posture. The garden was lonely. Over the house where she stood flew crows whose caw-caw reminded Bronagh as she worked of the blood of the African hunt. The baby had turned on its head and the suffering of birth was to come.

a banal stain

Yes, I was one of those who knew the house on Rue du Parc well. That's to say, I'm too young ever to have been there in its prime twenty or thirty years ago, in August, on one of the long weekends in May, or the ten days between Toussaint and the eleventh of November. Or again when the university took its February midterm break in the days when it still wasn't the done thing to jump on a train from Gare St Barthelémy to ski in the Alps. In its busiest, most glorious days, from the early nineteen-fifties to the end of the seventies, the house was hardly ever still. And yet this was the moment when, as Madame Darland herself showed me from some author's looping dedication in browning ink, family friends and acquaintances thanked her for creating at Rue du Parc 'a still centre of the turning world'. Take the oak staircase, wide enough for dignity and painted a friendly, rich cream. Imagine how in the past, the children of guests and visitors and close friends played there. In my day, the tail end of a hospitable era (for which hospitality we paid Mme Darland a nominal rent that went towards electricity and repair bills), those stairs were thin-carpeted, cluttered with dusty boxes of books and clothes in the sempiternal process of being sorted out. Undeniably, the original spirit, the *genius loci*, was letting go. In the gravelled drive weeds clustered drily and a round-roofed orange Peugeot rusted, abandoned by Mme Darland since her accident. Down into the back garden, the steps leading from the glass salon doors had cracked, would crumble. In the long grass a broken swing dangled on one chain, birds' nests collected for burning mouldered by the porch. Up in the attic, no doubt, boxes of letters and children's drawings dried to parchment under rolled, frayed carpets, cobwebs thickened theatrically into grey strings over broken toys, and dolls' eyes snapped open, glassily wide in the dark.

When the Darland daughters, Marie-Caroline and Odile, were growing up at Rue du Parc with their cousins and friends, the salon, painted that sky blue that recalls the royal fleur-de-lys cloth of the Louis, ebbed and flowed with a certain pragmatic sort of intelligentsia—marine scientists and biologists, eminent geologists and archaeologists, including the master of the house, Jean Jacques Darland himself, who when dying claimed to have stolen rocks from the moon. For the most part, they must have been a friendly lot. Their passion for their work placed them at one remove from the mephitic odours of the Second Empire bourgeoisie that permeated the ambiance of so much of early-twentieth-century France. They had travelled widely. Many were born in the colonies, most were familiar with French Africa, the Lebanon, Syria, the overseas *départements*, Martinique, Guadeloupe, the Île de la Réunion. Nearly all spoke another language, usually German. (The Germans had changed, Mme Darland liked to comment, making us all look at each other, while she watched the TV news. They were no longer at all those warrior Prussians with spikes on their helmets so hated by her Alsatian grandmother.) The Darland circle's reading had enlightened them to the etymology of the words they used; taproots and offshoots in Greek, Latin, Arabic or Persian. The long weekends and family parties often included Indochinese students researching doctorates at Parisian scientific institutes, medical doctors, lawyers from the Maghreb, mineralogists from Benin or Somaliland. The Darlands and their friends were believers in progress. With the Africans and the Arabs and the Indochinese, these academic, metropolitan French had memories and placenames in common, traditions and cooking smells from childhood, and, in the case of the black Africans, news of Brothers and Sisters from missionary parishes. I think of these houseguests of the Darlands, this Third World ascendancy, as the forebears of our dispersed, familyless student population, carrying our meals up the dusty stairs to share bottles of wine among half-finished dissertations in uncorrected French.

Maybe we who came in the end, the historyless ones (in their sense of a name attaching you to a line out of the past), maybe we even envied the Darlands' productivity. Their steady bookwriting, their enjoyable sense of rightness. Any dissidents in their milieu would have been professional religious thinkers who worked away their stay in the upstairs library overlooking the garden, there where I now slept on a small bed among empty shelves. They too would have eaten well-sauced meat dishes off the heavy silver service in the salon, the same joints and fillets that our Mme Darland, after a day's pottering around alarmingly heavy stone casserole dishes in the kitchen, still occasionally produced for us last ones. Us bits and bobs ended up at Rue du Parc through chance, and an unravelling web of Darland family connections. There were no lost ones in the old days, no outlaws or wandering souls—if you exclude the undiagnosed Alzheimer's to which Jean Jacques succumbed raving slowly, ordering dinner at 3 a.m., the shutters closed all day long to keep contamination out and facilitate his lunar rock-collecting expeditions. The daughters and cousins had grown up, and Bibi Darland refused to hire a nurse for her husband. During that long death what ideal took her through those years of slavery and despair? After Jean Jacques' death, the epitaph she had cut on his tomb was a quotation from a poet of her childhood: '*the ear that heard the best of me was closed off forever*'.

Sometimes Madame Darland mentioned the great Catholic philosopher Teilhard de Chardin. Her tone, the imperceptible inclination of the head when she spoke of this family friend, conveyed the sadness of finished mourning, resignation before the passing of all things, as in that biblical quotation they cite at funerals, 'in the morning of the day the grass springs up, in the evening it is cut down'. ('She's always thinking of funerals, she's terrified of dying,' said Ishmael, Odile's husband. 'Oh, I know what's coming, I know what's expected of me.' This, with an irritable jab of the shrivelled hand as if at a bothersome insect, was the nearest Madame Darland herself came to pronouncing on her own mortality.) One time when I was eating in the kitchen, she shuffled in and, not to impress but wistfully, in a movement of emotion, offered me a yellowed paperback, inscribed by the philosopher himself. Had she, Bibi Darland, given in marriage as a virginal seventeen-year-old, the way big, Catholic, aristocratic families gave a daughter to the Church, lived some sort of spiritual seduction by the great philosopher? Achieved some translation of her body to the noosphere in meditating the power of their unified love? Other names at Rue du Parc, apart from French politicians I did not recognize, included Captain Musset, an *habitué* before television popularized his charm. Marie-Caroline, the elder daughter, had famously complained of how Musset had dropped Bibi and the rest of the Darlands at the onset of their father's Alzheimer's. Nevertheless, somewhere a photo existed of the Captain's bony, charismatic smile among a group eating under the tree whose gummy spores, in my time, had stained and re-stained the white wooden table and chairs tipped onto it at the bottom of the garden.

It was Ishmael, married to Odile, the younger Darland daughter, who passed on to me most of these details of bygone seasons at Rue du Parc. Odile had 'found me' through the notice for the room to rent she had placed at Cité Universitaire. Ishmael was Algerian, a doctor, who had met Odile when he came to France for a year or two's specialization in his medical studies. They had two sons, Léo and Youssef. For reasons that I would later understand more precisely, when he brought his family to visit his mother-in-law Ishmael liked to seek out us other ones, the student lodgers, living frugally like cats in a museum among the gilded mirrors and marble fireplaces, the dignified light through the long windows. He was fond of opening up conversation, sharing a cigarette in the kitchen or on the broken steps into the garden. He had a way of abstractedly examining the bottom of his cigarette butt, with a doctor's eye for irregularity, as he spoke. To me Ishmael said that politically, the guests at the Darlands' would have been true-blue Gaullists. The men staunch, the women—a warning smile in my direction—for the most part conciliatory.

Ishmael liked to hear himself talk. He had already recounted to us how as a doctor in his own country he was used to having local politicians compete to buy his vote, which ensured the vote of the whole village. 'Let's not simplify,' he told us in one of the illuminations he liked to give us on France and French history. 'The past is not just another country, it's another culture.' These conversations usually took place on the broken steps outside the salon, while Madame sat inside with Odile. The grandsons, playing crocodiles in a river, careered around a tray of orange juice and chocolate *boules*. 'Remember, in Bibi's youth we are long generations before the student crisis of the sixties that divided this country into two camps: those who want change and those who fear for the future.'

I don't want to sound demeaning about the Darlands. The tenor of their life at the Rue du Parc must have been for the most part civilized, unviolent. For the outsider, the *invité* accepting his or her (mostly his) plate of *charcuterie* and sweet hock at the far end of the tables under the lime trees, those conversational afternoons in the garden must have seemed close to the companionable warmth of human society as it should be. Children playing, older venerables in their cushioned wicker seats, a tasteful proliferation of food and drink, Mme Darland's sweet dishes, her *religieuses à la crème* and her chocolate *boules*, still sold in patisseries as *tête de negres*, more successful than her Alsatian grandmother's veal's heads, tripe and sweetbreads. Imagine the *causerie* and debate in two or three different languages, the erudition, the genuine interest, think how the foliage and Lyonnaise birdsong, before the *train grande vitesse* netted all France to the boulevards of Paris, gave a utopian tint to these gatherings. Only a few days ago, while queueing for the library on the Place Nationale, I met a Laotian pharmacist who, on hearing I had lived for some time in the Darlands' house, suddenly lit up, out of the doldrums of a wet Lyonnaise afternoon. Didn't I remember, those Sundays in the Parc de la Tête d'Or with Bibi Darland? The picnics beside the *bassin* … surely I knew where he meant, the little lake, which they used as an ice rink in winter? He searched for the name, retrieved it smilingly from the past, like a chivalrous passerby picking up a dropped key or book … *La Grenouillère*! Hadn't I been on those picnics to *La Grenouillère*? There I broke in that I was too young, had only lived in the house after Mme Darland's accident and long after she had stopped going out, even to buy bread or post a letter—only to bite my tongue. For it was clear from the gentle pharmacist's nodding agreement that he saw my youth. He only wanted to talk. I am adding this anecdote to show how, despite what follows, the Darlands in their day, particularly Madame, understood how to provide a backdrop, some limelight, even a script for their sort of deracinated cultural protégés who were lonely in Lyon and France. Using this same analogy of a *mise en scène* to explain her system, Madame Darland herself used to say, 'I am only an influence in the wings. But an inescapable influence.'

Every so often, during my time at Rue du Parc when I was living in the disused library, 'young people'—they turned out to be in their forties or fifties but that was only half Mme Darland's life—rang up to remember themselves to her from the old days. She could rarely recall their names, which may have been result of the accident that had happened a few years after Jean Jacques Darland's death. Nevertheless, she felt beholden to these extras from the family *tableau vivant*. After these telephone conversations, she racked her memory for their biographies. She came to me, lavender mohair shawl drooping off one bony shoulder, her fine, little wrinkled hands against her face, the nails still manicured, fingers delicate and offputting, like a mouse's paws, her head to one side, appealing, blue-eyed, for me to help place some name in the house's past. In many ways the accident had left her as fragile, as dependent as a baby on the affection of others. Together, she hovering over a magnifying glass, we rifled through her boxes of letters, her photo albums and the tiny drawers of her *escritoires*. That was how, one afternoon, kneeling over a pile of papers in her 'den', I came upon memorabilia from the last war. Letters and newspapers from the occupation, documents in German and French. A broad pamphlet the size of a world atlas whose blown-up, thick-lined cartoon drawings, my eyes, my hands, like hers, touched lightly, passed over, following without thinking the gentle patting and putting aside of the little mouse sifting through old papers. Then in the dim light of her den, with its smell of tea and paper and pencil lead, and, as in a baby's bedroom, a not unpleasant close smell of sleep, kneeling there on the old persian rug at the black oak foot of what she called her worktable, my light boredom snagged, caught on a nail of understanding, focused, ripped slowly. I had taken in the title in teutonic script over the huge Punch and Judy nose of the cartoon sketch on the 'atlas', *Le Juif en France: Comment l'identifier sans se laisser tromper*. At my side Mme Darland opened a bundle of letters. Like waters or sands closing over a piece of evidence, the words were hidden again but not before the meaning had seeped out. 'French Jews, how to spot one and not be taken in.' There, crouched on the floor, I was living one of those moments that until then I had only read of, an illumination into the nature of things, ineradicable, like a mark burned into the skin. For the moment there was my student's incredulity weighted down, desensitized by the affection I had brought to her weakness, the endearing hesitations of her baby-blue eyes, the magnifying glass in the mouse's hand and the bent head balding under its chignon.

I was sitting on the cracking, mossy steps that led down into the garden from the salon and smoking a cigarette. I always went outside to smoke in the Rue du Parc. Any passage, however brief, in that house imposed attentiveness to some of the rites of olden days. A woman smoking was bad enough, the least that could be done was to retire outside if it wasn't raining too hard. Sometimes when I took a beer from the fridge or hurried outside, cigarettes in hand, I saw Mme Darland's blue eyes dip past me as if I were invisible. But then because I was not in her family nor even, for all she knew, in these ragtag and jetsam days of the end, from any *bonne famille* at all, she needn't concern herself morally. She hadn't seen me. But none of that mattered any more. I did not intend to stay on in the library upstairs, in this musty graveyard of an old world order. I no longer wanted to hear Madame Darland's shuffle in and out of the kitchen, or to watch from the upstairs window during a pause from my desk while she trailed her shawl after Minette the tabby into the long grass of the sunlit garden. I refused the half-chivalrous, half-alarmed care required of onlookers when, stiff and jerky as a marionette, she climbed on a velvet-topped stool and patted around the top of the bookcase for the tiny key that opened the china cabinet. Above all, I repudiated the memory of papers and documents soft with age on the ends of my fingers, the sight in my mind's eye, jutting out from under a pile of letters, of a thick-lined comic book. Just in time a friend on a study exchange in the States wrote offering to let me his room at the Cité Universitaire for the duration of his absence. I was going to leave the house in Rue du Parc.

Since then, the years have brought a thousand comments, revolving and thickening round that moment in the den with Mme Darland, though without obscuring it, as the drifting snow of time obscures other marks and voids. Who are we, goes one remark, not even born in the last war, to judge? How polite were the German soldiers in the street! Especially to women. How they stepped forward to open doors. And how was anyone to know? Mme Darland, too, voiced this last comment, though piteously, almost wringing her hands over words I later heard thrown out carelessly and with more sinister intent. How were they to know? Why think what the communists wanted us to think? How was anyone to know who exactly died? Everything had been cleaned up so cleverly, all the evidence tidied away.

'You know something?'

This was Odile, not Ishmael come to join me, stepping out of the salon onto the step where I sat. With her fingertips she balanced the french windows closed behind her so that my smoke would not filter back inside where Ishmael remained on duty with Bibi and the younger son, Youssef.

'I was just thinking, Bibi has changed so much.'

Odile is that rarity in France, a vegetarian, environmentalist. When I first met her, she said to me, 'I'm a human rights activist.' Oddly enough, this declaration did not make me as wary as most other statements of faith, *I'm a Jehovah's Witness*, for instance. Odile also has a doctorate in child psychology and worked in a government office on the Quai d'Orsay before taking on an advisory position in local Lyonnaise government. She crouched, frowning, thoughtful on the step beside me, the discomfort of her position a comment on my cigarette smoke. And also, despite the informality culled from summers in the States, the travelling in Africa with Ishmael, from a very French sense of place, hierarchy. Odile was a Darland, a daughter of the house, a mother twice over, an advisor in a government office. I was *de passage* at Rue du Parc. She did not require me to understand her loyalties. Mine, if any, were invisible to her, she did not ask any questions. For all these reasons, Odile could not sit down with the light, friendly clap on the shoulder, the wide grin of relief proffered by Ishmael when he came across me sitting on the garden steps or smoking a contemplative cigarette near the broken swing.

I ground out my smoke on the step, dusted off the ash stain with my fingers, and had the presence of mind to hold on to the butt rather than chuck it into the messy clump of weeds and lavender Ishmael and I used for that purpose. Odile's nondescript glance at my cupped hand told me that for the moment she was prepared to pass over knowing how we smokers at Rue du Parc usually disposed of our cigarette ends.

'What I am trying to say to you?'

She sighed, looked out over the early evening settling in the garden. Her English grammar was nearly perfect though her accent retained the Gallic singsong stress on the wrong syllables.

'It was our growing up that changed Bibi, it had to. You have to remember that Bibi was married (she said *marie'd*, like the name) as a girl, nearly a child. She knew nothing, *nothing* at all of the world!' Her eyes on my face widened into circles for emphasis. These were grey eyes. Odile had not inherited Mme Darland's doll blue. 'Bibi's parents protected her,' she grasped around for an expression, 'in ways we cannot imagine.'

'Overprotected.'

'Mollycoddled. That's right. They didn't let her go to school in case she caught *tuberculose*.'

I looked at her face, adamant under its unfashionable cap of red-brown hair. Odile at forty-something resembled her rosy-shouldered seventeen-year-old mother, in the portrait over the china cabinet in the salon, whose direct, unprovocative look made you wonder, Is this great simplicity or a tendency to plainness?

'So.' Odile let out a breath, sat down stiffly beside me. 'You see, I am upset to hear that you want to leave us, so quickly.'

I was taken aback but had my excuses at hand, an offer of a free room in the centre of town near the libraries, student economy and so on and so forth.

'But, we are so wor*ried* about Bibi. Since the accident.'

The acci*dent*.

'As I said to you before, we don't have to rent the room for money. The others'—she mentioned the other two students who rented upstairs rooms with me—'they are going home in the summer. We just need somebody to be with Bibi if she falls again. She might lie for days before we get to see her. Ishmael and I, we are so busy with the boys.' She shook her head, looked up at me with a quick, indrawn laugh. Her words were getting too close to confiding in a stranger. Nonetheless she had understood that this intimacy was necessary to keep me in the house. 'I know she's been saying the boys are too much for her recently. They tire her.'

The salon windows opened. We both turned to where Youssef, the youngest grandson, had appeared. Gingerly, with the toe of his grey sock, he was testing the top of the step like deep water. Odile and Ishmael's children had both inherited Ishmael's eyes. Their hair, cut in a neat bowl and shaved up to the ears like Shakespeare's princelings, was the colour of dark toffee.

'*Vas-y chéri, tu sors pas ici. Tu vas attraper froid. Va jouer et essaie de ne pas trop déranger Bibi.*'

She pushed him gently inside.

'It's not easy, to come here now. Sometimes we have to find a babysitter if Bibi is tired ...'

Does she know about those caricatures Bibi keeps in her *escritoire*, I wondered. If she does, why doesn't she make her mother get rid of them? Is it possible that she doesn't know? Is it possible that her mother, with that honed social sense of what should and shouldn't be said or shown, has never been as careless with her daughter as she was with me, about whose reaction she didn't care, that afternoon rifling among her papers? The Darlands' easy, practised hospitality, the gracious quiet of the library, had seduced me. And yet there was Ishmael's need to talk, to provide long explanations. Everybody knew. Everybody had always known what they would rather not know. Myself included.

Mme Darland had lived to see grandchildren half-Arab, Semites, like the Jews the good sisters in their blessed ignorance had taught them to pity at school. Ishmael had a story about how at the beginning of their marriage, Odile instructed her mother that Ishmael was agnostic, even 'religiously non-observant', but to no avail; Mme Darland knew his people had faith. 'In the event of war,' she said earnestly, famously, during one visit shortly after the wedding, 'of course we understand that your duty will be with your people, and Algeria.' She was sitting neatly, respectfully, knees pressed to one side, as she had sat before men all her life. She did not add 'against us in France'. By Ishmael's time, even Bibi Darland had learned that one had to adapt one's language to the times. The Church itself had changed. And that generation of Bibi's childhood had practically died out, along with those *bonnes sœurs* who applied the doctrine of deicide even to babies in the womb, like the embryo in Odile, who sat spluttering at her mother beside Ishmael's dark brows and semitic nose and broad smile, Ishmael pouring himself tea, extending a frail china cup to Madame. Mme Darland, ignoring her daughter's noises, accepted politely, her eyes shining very blue. Needs must. Her own grandchildren circumcised, half-Muslim. They had all learned their lesson; people need to respect their own cultures. Baptism no longer mattered. At school today children might chant '*café au lait*' but not '*Why did the Jews kill Christ?*'

'Please, let us count on you at least until the end of the summer,' Odile asked me that evening on the garden steps. The firm, confidential tones of the request sounded the government office at Quai d'Orsay, but her hand on my forearm was oddly stubby, the fingers strangely rounded, until I realized that she had bitten her nails savagely to the quick. The date, September, was important, she insisted on it. I thought, she wants me to understand that she is not asking too much of me, that it will be just this and no more. I was beginning to feel ashamed of my failure to see what was there, my need to fall under a spell that had been something to do with the weakness of Madame's thin hand, ropey with blue veins, adjusting the colourless hairs slipping from her hairpin. And also something more serious to do with needing to see history as a story book, a too great susceptibility to unused pink marble fireplaces, flaky wainscots, mirrors dreaming unseeingly, the conversations, the comings and goings of the past transubstantiated to morning air and sunlight …

'Just until the end of the summer. *La rentrée scolaire*? September. Then everything will get back to normal. *Tout va rentrer dans l'ordre*.'

Was it my imagination or in the days that followed was Mme Darland attempting to charm me, to win me over to her side of the question? Until then I had not even been aware of *sides*, but they existed and had ostensibly to do with the daughters, with Odile's and Marie-Caroline's attempt to protect Bibi from her own headstrong ignorance of her own frailty. The focal point of their fear and intensity remained obscure. I was sure their disquiet was not only to do with overprotectiveness for their Bibi 'after the accident', their fear of her little bird bones snapping, her rapid heart bursting between their fingers. There was a tone I could not identify in the raucous banter to which Marie-Caroline, the elder daughter, a gynæcologist with her own *cabinet*, married to Bruno (politician *Strasbourgeois*), subjected her mother during lightning visits to the house. Marie-Caroline was a small, sharp woman with her mother's blue eyes, who, if English, would have been horsy. As a tastefully dressed Lyonnaise, small-boned like Bibi, her horsiness was confined to her hectoring manner, probably very tonic for her patients in childbirth.

'There's Bibi off again,' she called out as Mme Darland hitched her shawl over her shoulders in a prelude to getting up

off the settee. 'Hey, everybody, watch Bibi's gymnastics now!'
Mme Darland, slipping into the kitchen to fetch a cake, slith-
ered under the force of her daughters' attention, clumsily
clutched a doorpost a split second from the disaster of her soft,
balding head on the tiles. 'Go on, give us a repeat performance,
Bibi,' cried Marie-Caroline as the gentle Odile, shaking her
head, came to lead her mother back to her seat.

'We don't belong—Thank God!—to a generation whose
women efface themselves with consummate grace for men and
children!' Marie-Caroline declared to me. She was the one
who showed me the silver shepherdess bell still hanging above
the couch where Mme Darland slept in the den. A stiff wire
connected the shepherdess to the library, now my bedroom,
where Jean Jacques Darland used to study all night. 'When it
rang, she jumped, *ma petite mère!*' said Marie-Caroline, in her
harsh voice, loud for Bibi's benefit. 'We're relying on you to
keep her in place!'—and there again was that note of insistence
I had heard in Odile's words on the garden steps and something else covered up, a valiant face put on somewhere and
Mme Darland smiling, showing all her elegant old teeth, and
pulling her mohair shawl over her bird breast. Her round blue
eyes gazed up at her elder daughter, much as her own mother
must have looked on smiling, unblinking, through clouds of
talk and tobacco smoke, in the salon, while every woman in
the room calculated how long it would take afterwards with
every window open to rid the walls and curtains of the nicotine smell that turned your stomach.

We were in the middle of the May month procession of long
holiday weekends: the *Fête du travail* on the first, *l'armistice du*

1945 on the eighth, *l'Ascension* sometime in the third or fourth week. On each holiday weekend families like the Darlands packed their cars and headed for their houses in the country or for relatives who lived outside town. In another lifetime the Darlands used to go to a place in the Dordogne. Madame's sketches and paintings of a pink granite house and stables hung on the walls of the wide stairwell. This year Marie-Caroline was driving her son Jean-Pierre, the eldest grandson, down to their boat at St Raphaël. Mme Darland took a lot of pleasure in relating all this to me. She really did have the capacity to forget that her own travelling days were now over, that like a toy with its mechanism kaput, she was relegated to a corner, forgotten in her box in the attic. She derived real pleasure from others' enjoyment. Ishmael and the other students had, on separate occasions, remarked to me on how much Bibi loved Jean-Pierre.

The May mornings stretched long and sunny. As if refracted through water rather than through the branches of the acacias and limes re-leaving, light rippled on the sky-blue walls of the salon, and on a seventeenth-century lacquered commode, which Madame, in her new winsome phase, opened out for me, revealing the painted riverbank inside the doors, the oval faces and geometric hairpins of Japanese courtesans kneeling and pouring tea. Humorously, she pointed out to me the table with cloven goat's hooves and hind legs sinuously rounded to accommodate the ladies' blooming crinolines. On my trips out to smoke on the garden steps, her eyes no longer slipped unseeingly past me. Once she even came close enough to explain in a flashing burst of disdain how the local council had warned her to keep a check on the cellar for damp rot. Damp rot! The houses in Rue du Parc had been

built over a stream which ran through the cellars for generations. But who today would be capable of distinguishing
between living humidity in a cellar, the cave heart of a green
mountain, and wet rot that undermines! No, after she was
gone (she spurned the future with that irritable jab of the
hand) and the water came back periodically, no one would
understand! Listening to her derision I understood that here
was the key to her personality. If the past is another culture, to
its mores alone did she pledge her loyalties; and as she said to
Ishmael shortly after his marriage, she did not expect fidelity
from any outsider.

On those early summer mornings I did not have to dash off
to the faculty library. I sat reading in the kitchen over a slow
breakfast and Mme Darland came shuffling across the mosaic
tiles of the hallway to talk to me, clapping her hands lightly in
the corridor outside the kitchen so I would not jump on suddenly meeting her round blue eyes when I looked up from my
book. Some of her chat on those mornings even skipped the
charm to cut close to the bone, as it were. Algeria, for instance.
In the salon, time and sunlight had faded a daguerreotype of
her father-in-law, an eminent archaeologist, unsmiling in
moustaches and frockcoat on an Algerian plateau. In the first
years of their marriage, Mme Darland had followed her husband to Algeria. 'It wasn't right, they never wanted us there,'
she said to me plaintively, in the kitchen. 'Oh, they didn't want
us and they made it clear. When we looked in their faces ...'
Her voice, pained, trailed off, conveying the disdain of the
young fruit-sellers and barrowboys, the women's eyes slanting
away from her, bearded men in djellabahs walking straight at
her past the walls of French villas with bare-breasted
Napoleonic figureheads. When she looked in their faces, there

must have been derisive intimacy, or hard displeasure, as if she should be punished for her presence on the pavement. Besides, despite the fresh oranges and dates and yoghurt, travelling in the heat among the adobe desert villages made her 'nause-ated'—a translation that leaves out the psychosomatic finesse of her own expression *mal au cœur*. I had been to Morocco so I could picture well the stifling sun and the warm sweat trick-ling down the furrow of her twenty-year-old back, smooth as the palm of a hand beneath the white cotton of a long dress, her fatigue in her wide-brimmed hat and tight shoes. Finally with Jean Jacques Darland, Bibi somehow, without confronta-tion, laid down the law. One of those ineluctable laws emanat-ing from the wings. 'Take me anywhere you like,' she conveyed to the face whose grey, oil-painted eyes gazed on us from a portrait in red magister's robes, 'I'll follow you anywhere in the world but not Algeria. Algeria's not right.'

The month of June bloomed full and heady against exhilarated blue skies over Lyon. Then in July the days grew stiller, colour-less with heat. The world was in the south of France and the children and grandchildren of the house at Rue du Parc scat-tered over the globe, Odile accompanying Ishmael to Montreal where he was attending a conference, Marie-Caroline and Bruno yachting in the Dom-Tom. In the house at Rue du Parc, Madame and I shared a quiet that was not a bad peace. Upstairs, among the empty boards of the library, the only movement was that of the light, and, in the August warmth, my concentration, a fluid calm, like the slow rise of bubbles in some liquid, perhaps ether. I was pleased with myself for, inspired perhaps by the industrious ancestral spirits at the massive leather-covered table where I worked, I was managing to finish a dissertation promised for late September. The most part of each day, Mme Darland slept away on her couch in the den. In the early morning and at lunchtime, her radio thrummed through my floorboards. I kept a wide distance from that room of even, papery quiet. She showed no signs of falling again as the family feared and appeared glad to be left to think of nothing at all. Or I did not want to see in what restless intricacy of past and present she was caught up as she sat late in the evening on the edge of the overgrown garden, intent and motionless, as if at the bottom of a deep, warm pool.

On the fifteenth of August, the *Fête de l'Assomption*, the summer reached its nadir, its deepest dip of heat and silence. Mme Darland's radio announced the beginning of the end of the season. Already thousands of motorists clogged the *autoroute du soleil* on the way back to the cities and towns of France for the *rentrée* at the beginning of September. Odile and Ishmael were due back from Montreal.

The telephone calls were the first interruption. Recently Mme Darland, pottering about in some far end of the house, had 'missed' her telephone calls, and as a result Marie-Caroline had had amplifiers fixed to the bell. Now when the phone rang, it seized the air in the house upstairs and downstairs mercilessly as an electric current, and our heads rang like anvils until, hands to her ears, Mme Darland finally teetered out to pick up a receiver.

That these first calls of the *rentrée* were angry I knew, not from eavesdropping, but because on coming downstairs one morning I overheard in Mme Darland's voice in her den the plaintive, sighing note she had used for Algeria. That tone she who preferred to guide from the wings allowed to escape her only under pressure of direct confrontation. Later, having finished my breakfast in the kitchen and read for a good hour uninterrupted, I glanced into the salon. There, in the fickle morning light, Mme Darland was sitting on the parquet, leaning against the wooden table with its goat's hind legs, beside the glass garden doors. Her eyes were lightly closed. The sun, horribly, had turned her baby head transparent, irradiating the blood in her pink skin, like wine held up to the light. I said her name. Her doll-blue eyes opened, focused on me. For the first few moments there was the expressionlessness, the unseeing slide of her disapproval. Then she smiled, dazedly, not looking at me. Her tiny, well-manicured hands went to her head. Opposite her the doors of the black lacquered Japanese cabinet stood open. She had been down on her knees, counting the cups and saucers, the glasses and cutlery, as she always did before family or old acquaintances arrived at Rue du Parc.

'Visitors coming?' I inquired brightly from where I stood. Unlike her daughters, I was not afraid for her.

'Ah yes, visitors …' She struggled up precariously, holding on to the edge of the table. 'You don't miss much, do you, up there, deep in your bookwork …' The look in her blue eyes then was challenging, spiked with dislike at finding herself so at the mercy of this young, forward foreign woman with nothing to recommend her, no name, no money, no marriage, no manners … *But none of that matters anymore today*, I addressed her mentally, holding my ground, returning her smile, *and anyway I'll soon return to what you see as the godless, cosmopolitan formlessness out there from whence I surged.*

Madame Darland, upright, her shawl pulled to, closed her eyes, touched her temple lightly. 'My grandson is coming,' she said. When she looked at me again, the usual old-age graciousness had softened her gaze. 'Jean-Pierre. You don't know him.' The mischievous look here meant, *This is one family detail we've managed to keep from you.* But she was recalling perhaps what she owed me, as a guest, and as a possible support for whatever familial tug of power was going on outside my knowledge. She prepared to charm me again, sacrificing, as so often in her long career, her personal tastes to the family good. I too played my part, coming in and closing the lower drawers of the Japanese cabinet for her, replacing on the shelves the gold-rimmed cups and saucers she had left on the parquet. Mme Darland had turned to the window and the yellow August immobility of the garden.

'When Jean-Pierre was a little boy I played with him there, really played. I used to pick him up, imagine the idea of me picking him up! I swung him by his ankles ... The others, Marie-Caroline, said, "Look, Bibi is playing, really playing, she's forgotten us!" My husband was working in the study up there, where you are now all day every day ... he'd put his head out the window to tell us to quiet down.' Thus, in some deft volte-face, she placed herself on the side of lawlessness and freedom, and me among the staid insiders.

Whatever my position, the return of the other Darlands meant my long stretches of concentration in the ancestral quiet had come to an end. The following day the phone clanged several times in that end-of-summer stillness. Again through the floorboards from Bibi's den came that note of contestation overheard on the stairs. I let it go. I was bent now on finishing my dissertation. If my days at Rue du Parc were numbered, I had no choice but to hold to my personal deadline and finish up the first draft before the hectic scramble for rooms at the Cité Universitaire, and this despite hearing from below the shufflings to and fro, the groan of a table displaced, a chair pushed lightly, the clinking of cutlery on plates. My Teilhardian bubbles of contained reflection, halted in their crystal ascent, were popping all around me. I threw my books into a bag and headed for the bus into the *bibliothèque nationale* to work on my concluding chapter. On my way past the kitchen, Mme Darland emerged. She wanted me to heave out the stone-bottomed saucepans from the cupboards under the sink.

Her manner had undergone a sea change since her hazy collapse on the salon parquet the day before. As I stooped to lift out the saucepans and cauldrons she used for her meat cooking, she stood beside me, shrivelled fingertips pressed obstinately together. Her hair, wispily disarranged from its hair-slides after that morning's furniture arranging in the salon, hung over one ear. But rather than turning her frail and transparent as on the previous day, the physical exertion had brightened her eyes, added a flush to her cheeks. She was telling me a story to which I was determinedly lending only half my attention. I had not forgotten the spiky dislike in those round blue eyes the previous morning and my decision to evade the webby antipathies of this old anti-semite. I wanted to get out of the house to the library and I wanted to see Odile and fix a date for moving out of Rue du Parc.

That morning Mme Darland was telling me a story to prove how Odile and the others were right to warn me about her, Bibi's, unpredictable nature. She had a tendency, she said meaningfully, to go against everyone's better judgement, 'to take in and shelter *all sorts of people*'. Once when Marie-Caroline and Odile were children and the new bus route had just extended to Rue du Parc, 'all sorts of people' started frequenting the area. Ex-prisoners. She paused and glanced up, though

I had not reacted. 'I always give them something, it's difficult for them when they've just been released'. Then there was this Moroccan woman and her child who knocked on everyone's doors asking for shelter, 'all henna patterns netting the hands and feet'. She showed me her own narrow, purple hands. Mme Darland had been alone in the house when she answered the door and she had taken them in immediately. Ensued the family reprobation, a questioning of her judgement, her husband's calling her 'unreliable'. To make amends, Mme Darland reflected that after all, this house belonged to the family, only one room was truly hers, and she moved the woman and her child into the shadowy ground-floor room they had always called 'Bibi's den'. To this very day, Marie-Caroline enjoyed telling the tale against her. 'There was really no knowing just what Bibi would do next!' She described how the woman sat gently smiling on the floor for a whole week, not doing much else but refuse to sleep in Bibi's couch-bed while her toddler played with Jean-Pierre's baby toys, some of which disappeared at the end of the week when a local organization found mother and child a hostel in town.

I straightened up with the last of the saucepans into the end of these reflections. Since her accident last year, Odile had said, Bibi had begun detailing her memories to exercise her mind. But I think they were wrong to see their mother at eighty-five as wandering among islets of light in the fog of memory. Mme Darland understood only too well the luminous energy of her own past. Standing head and shoulders above their Bibi in the kitchen, I saw a sight that widened my eyes. On the little formica table at which I usually ate behind a propped-up book, stood an array of dark, dusty bottles, a good ten years' worth of burgundies, vintage whites and reds, whiskies, brandies and—

the procession continued under the table—dusty-shouldered cognacs and explosive-looking vodkas. That explained the repetitive shuffling back and forth I had heard from my desk upstairs. Madame watched me with a glint in her eye. She had spent all morning transferring the contents of the drinks cabinet locked in one corner of the salon.

'I decided it's safer to move them,' she said. 'Into the larder. Or the cellar.'

I knew I had to hold out against the alarm word 'cellar', planted with some deliberation. For Mme Darland's startlingly dangerous descents down the slippery spiral stairs to fetch a tin, or to follow Minette the tabby, constituted one of her worst sins of recklessness in the eyes of Odile and Marie-Caroline. I left for the library.

When I came back to the Rue du Parc late that evening there were voices in the salon. Downstairs, the air was flavoured with the thyme and fatty perfume of a finished platter of *gigot d'agneau*, and through the double doors left ajar I noted on the table an uncorked St-Emilion, no doubt opened for Ishmael's benefit. Odile, like her mother, consumed only thimbles of alcohol on special occasions. Odile was there now, talking, firmly, like a teacher explaining something precisely once and for all. In some puzzlement, thinking Ishmael mustn't be back in Lyon yet, I put my head round the salon door. Everyone knew that soft-hearted Odile always let Ishmael do any serious talking to Madame Darland, who only listened seriously when the speaker was a man. But Ishmael himself was there in person, seated under the oil-portrait of Jean Jacques Darland in red robes. Ishmael was exerting his calm on little Youssef, hunkered over, concentrating on a toy at his father's feet. Odile gave me a sideways look of recognition and went on talking to her mother. Seated on a *chaise longue*, bony knees together like in the daguerreotypes of her childhood, Madame Darland's whole person wore the shuttered, neutral expression which meant *You all have opinions that make each other angry, you suffer and make others suffer. I, Bibi, listen and say nothing.* Ishmael, his hand restrainingly on his son's head, briefly turned on me his wide, glad smile. I indicated to him the cigarette pack in my hand. With a jump of relief, I understood how good it was, after all these weeks with Mme Darland, to be greeted in this house as an equal and not some mysterious and lesser dependant. And now with Odile back in Lyon and the conclusion to my dissertation nearly written, the moment had come to leave the silence of the past to find its own level in the past's play of dark and sunlight on those sky-blue walls.

Ishmael, his smile dimmed from some strain, maybe the weariness of travel, joined me on the broken garden steps with an unlit cigarette in his hand.

'How was Montreal?'

He shrugged, lit up. 'Work. Hard work. And *your* work?' He turned to me, his eyes suddenly complicitous.

'Good. I've made a lot of progress.' I realized he meant Mme Darland. 'But she's … as always. I don't understand all this caution, the fear I sense among you.'

Ishmael made a noise through his nose, turned away and flicked ash into the dusk over the weedy clumps of lavender.

'It's Jean-Pierre they're afraid of.' He used Mme Darland's phrase, 'You haven't met him yet. The winters he's normally in South Africa or Swaziland. He's got an import-export thing going on down there.'

We looked at each other ironically. These were the days of full-blown apartheid.

'August is a problem because he's here in Lyon. Marie-Caroline is always talking about the studio flat they've invested in for him but he never uses it. Bibi's the only one who will take him in. Marie-Caroline and Dili don't want her to put up with him.'

'He's the black sheep, then,' I said.

The corners of Ishmael's mouth turned down in a show of indifference. Unseeingly he studied the nicotine stain on his cigarette filter. 'They worry because he's a heavy drinker. And he throws things around when he drinks. As a youth he was in the Front National, young lout section, poster of Hitler in his bedroom, did a couple of months' prison for beating up little *métèques* like me. Oh, every family has its *jardin secret*.' He laughed, looking ahead of me into the garden where the sun had set. Under the sticky tree trunks by the Darlands' old garden table, the olive-coloured light held still as a candle flame in a shrine.

A noise came from behind us. Ishmael glanced back through the salon doors and saw my expression.

'I haven't had any trouble with him. He's fine with me, is Jean-Pierre. He's not stupid, although he still has some very rough friends, but that's to annoy Marie-Caroline. We'd get on well if Dili let him come to the house.'

He then told me some stories about Jean-Pierre, his getting drunk and trying to throw his mother out the window. 'Marie-Caroline's a toughie and some of her ideas are not so far from her son's, but I don't think she'd bounce.' He told me about his turning up in the car to take Youssef and Léo to picnic in the Parc de la Tête d'Or—'you know where Bibi used to go on her

Sundays?'—and his rage when Odile, out of fear, refused to let her children go.

'All that was before my time here,' I said.

'Yes?' He was looking back again over his shoulder into the scene in the salon.

'The problem with this family is they make each other worse,' he said. As if to confirm his words, rapid steps crossed the parquet inside. Odile opened one of the glass doors and said, ' 'shmael, I'm taking Youssef back now.' Her face was averted so obviously I looked up in surprise and saw she was crying. Tears brought her out in pink and red blotches as though she had been slapped in the face.

Ishmael's expression changed abruptly. He reached up and took her wrist, a movement that broke in her a burst of explanation: 'She keeps saying that it's nothing to do with me, that I know nothing. I don't know what goes wrong when I try to talk, I was only trying to help her. If anything should happen to her ... and Bibi, she got up and walked away from me. *Glaciale*! She kept saying it was nothing to do with me, as if I'm too young or too stupid to understand.' She put away Ishmael's hand from her wrist, sniffed and wiped her nose with a balled-up handkerchief. 'You stay on awhile,' she said to him, her voice quietened. And then she left us, shutting the salon door behind her. I glanced at Ishmael. He had thrown his cigarette away and was sitting forward, thinking, his long, lean-fingered hands against his face. From the salon an oblong of lamplight stretched into the grey of the garden. Finally, Ishmael with a tired expression of irritation made a move to get up. 'What goes wrong? What goes wrong?' he said, imitating his wife wearily. 'They don't know, they don't want to know what to see in that ... soft, old lady's ...' He looked around for

a word, 'bald head'. In that comic emphasis was the flinty bit-
terness for the enemy identified, absent when he spoke of
Jean-Pierre's brutality. 'She has it in her, Mme Darland, to
outwill them all.' He stood up, dusting his hands, went on
explaining with the didactic tone he couldn't resist, 'They forget that this was the woman who in 1968 stayed at her husband's side during the student riots in Paris. This little ...
birdlike woman took her husband's arm, accompanied him to
the Sorbonne.' He stepped down towards me to accept another
cigarette, waved the hand that held it towards the invisible
garden to evoke the scene.

'Imagine! Arm in arm across the picket lines, the barri-
cades, the tear gas, under a hail of cobblestones ...' He spoke
very seriously, then shook his head and laughed, paused to
light his cigarette. Then he opened the salon door, walked over
the parquet, smoking casually in flagrant breach of the decorum at Rue du Parc.

One consequence of Odile's tears was that, unable to put to her
there and then the question of my moving, I was still in the
house a week later when Jean-Pierre arrived. It was late, after
dark. I had been sitting dully with a book propped up against
a teapot at the kitchen table, when a key sounded roughly in
the front door lock. In a rush of cold air and cigarette smoke,
Jean-Pierre let himself into the house. 'If they knew he had a
key!' I exclaimed inwardly, peering with interest through the
interstice of the kitchen door-hinge. My vantage point from
the kitchen table was just right for seeing without being seen.
Mme Darland, who had been moving with a discordant hum
between her den and the salon, her mohair shawl trailing off

her shoulder and her head empty, had long forgotten my presence behind the kitchen door. I saw a dark, handsome head,
short, stocky legs, oddly light-coloured eyes in a swarthy,
unshaven face. Attractive, but repulsive because of what they
had told me. Jean-Pierre took his cigarette out of his mouth to
kiss the top of his grandmother's head.

'Are you well, Bibi?'

'Here you are at last,' said Mme Darland, her voice trembling. Her grandson took off his coat, flung it across a chair
and went into the salon, calling over his shoulder, 'Come and
say hallo properly, Bibi.' The self-assurance of his movements
disorientated her. Mme Darland pulled her heavy shawl tightly
over her chest and I knew she was remembering the pressure of
the bottles she had stored away from him in the kitchen. She
jerked guiltily, a marionette tugged in two directions, then she
shuffled after him, dragging her shoes, as if too tired to lift her
feet properly. The double salon doors remained open into the
hall. Jean-Pierre had thrown an open packet of cigarettes on
the dining-room table beside a slab of newly baked chocolate
cake that had been waiting since that morning in its silver foil
beside teacups and plates. He sat biting a thumbnail. Madame
Darland must have glanced worriedly at the cake, for I heard
him say, 'I had something to eat in town, Bibi, don't bother
yourself,' as he reached over the table for his cigarettes.

'Oh, I know you don't come here to eat my cakes,' she
answered quickly. One family complaint was that Jean-Pierre
used Bibi as a free restaurant when he couldn't be bothered to
cadge a dinner elsewhere. The exaggeratedly tired note in her
voice surprised me; she was using it, unconsciously or not, to
hold him at bay. The quiet between them boded ill. Uneasi-
ness, even recriminations withheld, swirled in the blue smoke

over the chocolate cake and the lacquered eighteenth-century Japanese women who, on their riverbank forever pouring tea into flat cups, understood the importance of listening and arranging behind the scenes. Mme Darland lifted a corner of her shawl to her eyes, which watered easily. Like Odile she was allergic to cigarette smoke. I was waiting for them to get talking so that I could slip out of the kitchen and upstairs. But Jean-Pierre lay back in his chair, stretching out his short legs and contemplating the smoke curling between his thumb and forefinger, and when he talked it was slowly, with long spaces between the phrases.

'I tried to give up last week, you know, Bibi,' he said. 'It didn't work. Sick as a dog I was. All day. Couldn't remember a thing afterwards. My mind was a black hole. Everything zapped, kaput.' He got up, boots sounded on the parquet. 'It was frightening,' his voice came back, self-assured and offhand. At the same moment, Bibi in the salon and I, watching from the kitchen, both realized that he was about to discover the empty drinks cabinet. My heart beat hard; their fear after all was contagious. Very quietly I stood up, book in hand, remembering the hopelessness in Ishmael's sigh, *In this family they make each other worse*. In the salon, Mme Darland had also struggled to her feet. Withered, weightless, her hands moved vaguely, she patted her pockets again as if searching for something forgotten, some hard essential that had slipped from her mind like a key or a ring down a grating. At last Jean-Pierre reappeared, holding a flat crystal cognac flask, which he turned upside down, and then held the viscous beads on the bottom up to the light.

'Still a tad left.' He looked down and around the room as if the missing bottles might be stacked somewhere on the floor or under the dining table.

'I'll get you something from the kitchen', said Mme Darland, wavering, gripping her shawl.

'No, don't move, Bibi.' From where I stood, the phrase sounded toneless, innocuous, but Mme Darland took the words as an order. She actually tried to freeze, the way children do in a game of statues, and in the very intensity of her effort she knocked clumsily back against a chair.

'Thanks for trusting me, Bibi,' Jean-Pierre muttered darkly. I could not imagine the expression in those round, blue clockwork doll's eyes before him. Distraught? Pleading? Hands clasped with the desire to undo, to repair?

'When you are here your mother holds me responsible for you,' she began, and her voice was more piteous than I had ever heard it in my time in the house.

Jean-Pierre banged the cognac flask on the table. 'They want me locked up, Maman and Odile. You know that, Bibi!' he shouted. I stared at the stocky figure and his light-coloured eyes, surely they were bloodshot. Now, before he hit her, I was going to walk across the hall and say some neutral thing, or maybe it was better to call out from where I sat.

Jean-Pierre kicked a chair over and howled, 'That's their "responsibility" for me! Sending me "somewhere run by people trained to cope with my sort of personality". You know that, don't you!'

'I know, I know,' said Mme Darland, gravely, as if what he had said was of tremendous importance. And in fact, some significance which escaped me had just been expressed, for in the next moments the scene before me transformed itself, as if a multitude of words and gestures, a long passage of time, had been collapsed into a few instants. Decorous as her sisters, the eighteenth-century Japanese tea courtesans, Mme Darland sat on the chair she had knocked against in her fear. There she waited, rickety legs and ankles ropey with blue veins pressed together, transparent hairs slipping from their pin. Only the eggshell head tipped to the left threatened to tilt too far as she observed Jean-Pierre, talking and shaking and exhaling smoke.

'These people don't know how to be responsible for their own fucking lives, look at Maman, she'll die before you, Bibi, she's so stressed up! Odile with her fucked game of love for all. Of course you, Bibi, have to please everyone. Take care not to offend Odile, human rights expert, and her brood. You're all the same ...' Just as I decided to creep upstairs and phone Ishmael, his violence broke on some futility, like the exhaustion of a child who has come through a tantrum.

He sat at the table, his head in his hands, his mouth twisted with displeasure, and then leaned forward over the table, rested his head in his arms. At last, his voice low, he said, 'I must be sick to yell at you like that.' Motionless at my post in the kitchen, I breathed again. Now spells of silence broke up their murmurs to each other, they had found again a rhythm familiar to them. Crossing the hallway to the stairs, I heard Jean-Pierre's words: 'This country is sick. I have to get away, Bibi. It's rotten to the core, especially in winter, Bibi, there's no movement here, nothing, it's a morgue.'

I was too far up the stairs to hear the end of this muttered plaint. From his presence on the following evenings, however, I can reconstruct what happened later between them, after I finished reading and snapped my light off upstairs.

From the kitchen, Mme Darland fetched a glass, a small bottle of tomato juice and two thumb-sized plain glass pepper and salt cellars. Shuffling over the parquet with her tray to where Jean-Pierre lay stretched on the *chaise longue*, she bent laboriously to leave the tray on the floor, then sat beside him on a straight-backed velvet-topped chair under the daguerreotype of his grandfather on a pink Algerian plateau. In a few hours he would sleep, turned on his stomach, head on one bent arm, the other hand open, uncurled. An adult hand, the palm callused, the fingers nicotine-stained and the nails, like Odile's, bitten to the quick. Sometimes when he slept, Mme Darland left the salon windows ajar, to get rid of the cigarette smell. After the white August heat of the day, transpiration rose from long grass and untended plants, scented as if from a nectary. Into the early hours of the morning Bibi Darland waited and kept watch. Sometimes Jean-Pierre woke up and called her. He always slept with the light on; I already knew from Ishmael how he had bad dreams—an alcoholic's dreams, populated with repulsive creatures that converged on him. Exactly how long through the night Mme Darland sat on and on, balanced hunch-backed on the hard chair, dozing, waking with a tremor, her narrow, child-sized hand rising to press the thin hair above her ear, is not clear. The last achievement of her engineered frailty was this stubborn vigil kept with her eldest grandson, the endpoint of eighty-five years' *éducation comme il faut.* 'Blood is thicker than water,' she once said to me. 'The others, Odile especially, so ready to defend other ways, other tastes, forget to respect their own.'

Finally, through Ishmael, I managed to put a number on my days at the house in Rue du Parc. During these last days with Mme Darland I had ample opportunity to observe what Odile and Marie-Caroline called Jean-Pierre's base selfishness with his grandmother. When she floundered around in the kitchen preparing his food, struggling insect-like with the cooking implements from another age, he turned the volume up on the TV he had installed in the wide hall between the kitchen, Bibi's den and the salon. Likewise, his thumb-biting, abstracted concentration on game shows or football matches never wavered when, balancing on the slippery cellar steps and chut-chutting impatiently at the cat, Lolotte, who wound confusingly round her ankles, his grandmother disappeared for a disconcerting length of time. Maybe when she resurfaced, cat banished, tin in hand, breathing quickly, wisps of hair fallen unequally over her face, mohair shawl trailing like a dead wing, swerving towards the kitchen, he straightened up, or otherwise changed position in his armchair. He never wondered if she was sleeping or eating enough. He left ashtrays overstuffed with twisted butts on the stairs or floor where she was certain to trip.

Odile and Ishmael steered clear of Rue du Parc for the duration of Jean-Pierre's occupation. Jean-Pierre's parents, Marie-Caroline and Bruno, if they knew what was going on, made no sign. Then one morning, not long after his arrival, the phone clanged; Mme Darland was out somewhere in the long grass of the garden, so to silence the gonging amplifiers I reached for the receiver.

'Poor Bibi, did I wake you?' boomed Marie-Caroline, and charged on, stentorian as ever, 'Now, about Jean-Pierre, we've spoken to him, Bruno and I, and we made it clear to him that he is not under any circumstances to come and bother you. He should be perfectly able at the age of twenty-nine to find himself somewhere to sleep, if the flat we bought him is not to his taste. You do remember we bought him a flat, are you listening, Maman?'

She paused at last. I hesitated, then introduced myself.

'Ah. Marie-Caroline here,' she said. 'You realize that he's not telling the truth when he says that he's got nowhere to go.' Her voice rose. Here was the splinter in Marie-Caroline's heart. She could not bear Jean-Pierre saying he had nowhere to go. I imagined her eyes shiny, the cheeks with a dot of red as Ishmael had described her at family gatherings where they plotted 'to send Jean-Pierre somewhere with people trained to deal with his sort of personality', and Marie-Caroline, her eyes burning with the determination of a woman touched to the quick, joined in with tales of all the money spent on her son.

She demanded, 'Tell me, did he ring up?'

'No, no,' I said, truthfully. He hadn't telephoned before turning up at the house. 'At least not while I was here,' I added, unnecessarily.

In more subdued tones, for she had taken in the fact that she was talking to an outsider, Marie-Caroline said, 'Remember, we're prudent because we all know how he tires Bibi out, that's all.' She finished off and hung up on the conversation as abruptly as she had begun.

A year or so after that, Odile rang me at my apartment in north Lyon to tell me that Madame Darland was in hospital. She had fallen, of course. The inevitable, disastrous crack of that soft, balding head on the mosaic tiles of the hallway that they had lived out so fearfully thousands of times, as often as Shakespeare says a coward lives out his death. Only 'the brave ... die but once'. I thought of that withered hand jabbing the air as alluding to her own dying, of her saying, 'I know what's coming', and I wondered if she was finding enough bravery for 'what was expected of her'. By the time I got round to visiting, her condition had deteriorated badly. The journey took hours, for the public hospital where they had put her was at the industrial suburban end of a new metro line. She had been in a coma and was now in a half-vegetative state, maybe alert, maybe not, usually curled up fœtally on her side, the violet-coloured mouse hands gripping stubbornly—or uncontrollably—the raised bar of her cot. On the two or three occasions I journeyed out to see her, she was not in a good mood. Squeezing her face up with dislike, or futile, hysterical protest, she turned her head obstinately away from me on the pillow, clung so hard to the cot rails that a nurse had to come and prise off her fingers to stop her hurting herself. Most confusingly, for I was sure in the house at Rue du Parc she had retained all her brownish, elegant teeth, her mouth had caved in and was now empty of all but four long, witchy molars which she ground continually, scrunching up her yellow eyelids, in a caged, desperate movement that accentuated despairingly if I tried to take her hand or talk to her.

On a little side table with a display of family photographs, Odile had organized a visitors' notebook. None of us believed Bibi Darland had long to go. But she lived for months, through one winter, a spring and a summer and well on into the beginning of another *rentrée scolaire*. 'Her heart is strong,' Ishmael said to me. 'It's often the case at the end of a long, healthy life. The heart won't give up. If she loses consciousness, they might pack her in ice.' Jean-Pierre, now settled in the house on Rue du Parc, came to her bedside every day. It was he who had found Bibi on the floor outside her den and had called the ambulance.

I didn't go to the funeral but, as is French custom, to a sort of memorial wake held at Rue du Parc for second-degree friends and acquaintances of the Darlands and the house. There, Ishmael told me he and Odile and the children were moving to Casablanca; 'Come and stay with us there,' he said, offering as usual his glad, friendly smile, but he forgot to give me their address before he left. Jean-Pierre was off to South Africa with a taciturn and tightly miniskirted girlfriend. Marie-Caroline, kneeling in the den, said, 'The house will go for some four and a half million.' Earlier, the shocked look in her eyes which suddenly looked very round and light blue, like Madame Darland herself peeping out over her daughter's harsh words, had moved me. How had I failed to notice the resemblance between Marie-Caroline and her mother? Had this death undone the elder daughter's face, stamped it with face of the lost mother, as if on a molten coin? I would have liked to think of that osmosis of past and present come to an end. I didn't bother walking through the rooms. Someone had cut the shifting branches in the garden and put an end to that butterfly dance of light and absence of my summer in the library. From the cellar to the attic there were drawers and commodes to be emptied and sorted into the piles for burning and keeping. In the steady daylight flooding the rooms, a certain stoniness announced winter.

a recitation
of nomads

'Pourtant je partirai (serais-je déjà parti?)
Parti reviendrai-je?
Et si je partais? Et si je ne partais pas? Et si je ne revenais pas?'
—Jean Tardieu, *Conjugaisons et interrogations*

They were sharing a couple of narrow but sunny rooms under the roof, refurbished servants' rooms with wooden beams, near the quartier St Paul and the bridge over the Seine at Sully Morland. He had got them the place cheap, off a friend of a friend who was going back to New York after five years in Paris.

Soon these rooms took on for them the strength of presence of a living being. Everyone who climbed to this eyrie of theirs, up six flights of polished, carpeted stairs through a faint ground-coffee scent, past double oak doors of parqueted, house-sized apartments, up to the sixth floor where the carpets and oak gave way to dusty, unpainted boards—everyone admired the atmosphere they had created in their place. They had filled the two rooms with bright colours and chosen plants and furniture and rugs like the ingredients of a simple meal carefully prepared to please the other. In this first 'pampering stage', as he privately referred to it, they were playing a chil-

dren's game of making a shelter. He brought up a Latin
American basket rocking-chair, which they tipped against the
wall when they rolled out their futon, and a Turkish kilim,
hand-woven in lopsided rectangles of gypsy colour, offered
him in lieu of payment for English classes. One Friday night
walking in the alleys of the second-hand antique shops around
St Ouen, she found a round, short-legged, wooden table balanced on a stack of bin bags and leavings from the flea market
at Porte de Clignancourt. He cooked for her with fruit and
vegetables from the cheaper street markets. She fed and
watered a ficus tree by the window and tended spidery shoots
of aloe vera plants a friend of hers had brought back from wild
scrub growing on roadsides in Sicily. Over the narrow mantelpiece of a brown-veined marble fireplace she hung her dense
pencil sketches. Outside, the grey roofs and boulevards of Paris
stretched without horizon into an austere sky.

Neither of them had been born here. He had drifted to Europe
after growing up in a family of teachers and doctors in
Chattanooga, Tennessee, then a diploma from film school
somewhere outside Boston, followed by a year with a swami in
California, followed by wanderings in Chile. There he was
marked. In Santiago he had had a girlfriend whose family
members had died in prison or fled the country. Like one of
those relationships in a Bob Dylan song, she talked to him of
revolution then left him to go to California and major in history of art. Next, in Peru for a little over a year, he taught
English in a missionary school in the mountains. In Paris he
was working on a film script based on both these last experi-
ences, the Chilean girl and the school.

She, after three years of a flamboyant, prestigious art school in London, had been unable to stick 'an urban work routine'. She had motorbiked in Australia, caught some virus in Indonesia. This last he believed. She was thin to the point of emaciation. She smoked non-stop. She lived off tea from a mug with one dunked teabag and condensed milk from a tube rolled up like toothpaste. Her very thin blonde hair was chin-length, streaked white, whether naturally or not he never knew; her small, serious face with its densely freckled Anglo-Saxon skin stopped imperceptibly short of prettiness. She carried with her an aura of being on the run, sometimes affected a lethal resignation he hated. She had cut from her family. Yet in the photograph she showed him, her parents, northerners (there was a touch of northern English? Scottish? in her accent that had struck him at first as very uppity Brit), did not look the sort of hicks he knew from the States, the rednecks living out their lives dumbly in front of the TV screen like patients in a lock-up ward. She had some story about a sister and drugs he had not yet gone into. In the words he wrote for his main character, Anna, drop-out art student and teacher in a missonary school in Chile during the coup d'état of the mid-seventies, 'to each his own dark images that might swell and break them, or splinter and bleed them dry'. He would have cast the young Meryl Streep for Anna, or Isabelle Huppert.

In Paris, they had each been on their own before they met at an overcrowded party given by an Irish teacher of English near Bastille. He had got there with friends of friends who disappeared. Somebody gave him a joint which he finished and then he drank a lot of wine very quickly. Music and smoke and whirling drunkenness slammed and ebbed contusingly, working without success towards some psychedelic reversal of things, a skyscrapered landscape coming and going against the sea. Soon the floor was wet and trodden with cigarette butts, like a public toilet. At an open window people he would later meet again with her were talking with druggy intensity about commitment to articulating the silences in the language. He was surprised; the scraps of psychoanalysis and structuralism picked up in his film school had led him to expect more cynicism from Europeans. She said she was a painter. He got very happy, as usual when he drank. Full of unspent tenderness, he kept putting his arm round her skinny shoulders and pulling her towards him. Someone opened the window and sang into the sleeping courtyard, '*Je vous salue Paris, plein de merde. Le fruit de vos entrailles est pourri.*' Towards four o'clock, the police arrived. They left together, he and she, along with some others. She was smoking and coughing. At the door they ducked a woollen cap being passed around for contributions to the two-thousand-franc fine imposed on those living in the flat.

'Never met any of the guys that live here,' he said, grinning his healthy smile at her. She shrugged, very dry and unflirtatious. She gave him details. The girl's mother was a writer, though her books weren't selling; the boyfriend, that much older British guy in a thin, beige raincoat worn open over his shirt and trousers, had lived for years with a woman in a Palestinian refugee camp.

'Uh-huh?' he said politely.

They walked through the first, whitish light and the pneumatic whish of the streetcleaners' little green vans spraying the empty pavements. The air, after the heat and smoke of that party, smelled as wholesome as baking bread. Soon on the quays by the slowbacked Seine he wanted to holler and whoop, *Je vous salue Paris!*—but he held himself back, looking at her feathery hair, her hands pushed into the back pockets of her black jeans skinny-tight against her narrow buttocks.

'Everything in its proper place,' he murmured, though the phrase was not right. Looking at her did not bring on that on-the-tongue foretaste of an objectively voluptuous woman. And yet as she walked ahead of him, ungenerous, muffled in the sort of puffed-up ski jacket he disliked, he had to keep on looking for whatever it was in her that had been sharpened to a point, worked out of joint. She probably wore the jacket to hide her boniness. He had decided that that self-contained, unattached style of hers, which veered from non-committal to jarring, was what he needed to counter his big, friendly, laid-back attitude. Perky, unaccommodating resistance, that was what set him off.

They were living without much money. He was working on his script during his *petit boulot* as a night security man in a two-star hotel on the Avenue de la Grande Armée. She was sick of teaching English so at weekends she sold cheap clothes on a street-market stand in the suburbs. When they had spare cash left over from cinema tickets, they drank beer and ate *moules frites* in an airy brasserie, l'Oiseau Bleu, whose pale blue walls, tulip-shaped ceiling lights and spacious leather seats gave out an American feel of worn, jukebox kitsch foreign to Paris. As a sign of their entry into coupledom they grew habits like sitting at a round table by the open-air terrasse of l'Oiseau Bleu. They sat there smoking Gauloises Blondes over their empty glasses, as long as the waiters would let them stay without ordering. At the beginning of the afternoon, lunchers from offices and shops roundabout crowded the horseshoe bar behind them, the tables filled with workers eating sandwiches, drinking beer and wine and coffee. The drinkers standing at the bar smoked heavily, dropping the butts on the floor under the nickel foot-rail, oblivious to a huge indolent Alsatian that lay on the floor beside the brass cash register. Then as the crowd thinned, the waiters started cleaning the tables, replacing salt and mustard cellars, crumpling wine-stained paper tablecloths. The steak-and-sauces smell faded into a stale cigarette haze and the rattle of the pinball machine. They got up and left, to walk through the poor areas, Chateau Rouge and Max Dormoy in the north of Paris, along one of those boulevards where the metro overground near the heavily policed immigrant area of the Goutte d'Or blocked out all but a strip of sky overhead, and there was always an odour of poverty secreted in the fish leavings and fruit and vegetable remains trodden by the crowds of the street market at Barbès Rochechouart. Once, a young Arab woman wandered uneasily in the Saturday afternoon traffic, ringed by aggressive *flics*, their hands on their guns. She was wailing, 'What's it to you if I wanna die?' Arabs and Africans stopped to watch on the pavement, waiting for the police to put a hand on her, or insult her, so that they could take her part ... Up at the Sacre Cœur, Japanese schoolgirls laughed hysterically as pigeons alighted in their hundreds to feed on the bread they crumbled, and laughed again in screeches when two American youths stopped by their bench and tried to pick them up. In good weather they sat in parks, or squares overhung with sun-dried chestnut trees, and drank beer, usually 1664 from tins. When the summer dog days, the *canicule*, stifled the city, they rode the metro out to the countrified greenbelt around the city, never buying tickets and always sitting by the doors to pre-empt the ticket inspectors with their notebooks who patrolled the trains in gaggles of four or five looking to make commissions on fines. Of course, they learned each other's mythologies. He talked a lot about South America, where he had spent two years out of twenty-nine. She referred more than she knew to her childhood. He saw the little girl in her, spoiled by her father, a bossy, dreamy, strong-willed little girl who imposed what she wanted on those around her.

She cleared one of their two rooms to work at a series of miniatures she had had in her head before she met him. She said, 'I mustn't let myself be distracted.'

'You mustn't. Enough of this wandering around like two kids skipping school. Sneaking into cafés for ill-afforded liquor.'

'Smoking on park benches.'

It was also agreed that they had got into eating too much from the fast-food stands. He went back again early in the morning to the street markets at Villiers and Barbès and refilled the cupboard and fridge with fruit and vegetables. Also, intending to revisit his scenario of revolution in Latin America, he bought himself some pens and notebooks. On the inside front cover of one of the notebooks he wrote these sentences paraphrased from a Conrad novel: 'A revolution happens when there is no legality, no institutions, nothing worth reform, just a power that represses ideas, defends its own existence …'

These words pleased him for their disgust, the disenchantment in them. Ideals betrayed. Where, he wondered, in the history of western Europe and America, or in his own life for that matter, had he lost his ideals? Where had a bargain been struck to exclude, along with the dirt and brutality he had witnessed in Chile and Peru, these peaks and depths of moral intensity? Safety and security. He had no illusions. The people he came from had negotiated, it was well known. He looked at history and knew he belonged to the privileged caste who had left it to others to pay the price for that freedom which was their inherited condition.

That spring, their second, she woke one morning during the first warm days of March with what she later described to him as a 'buzzing numbness' in her head that she took for the beginnings of a bad cold. Dry-eyed she sat up in bed in the liquid yellow sunlight for which they had longed through the muddy skies of the last four months. Half asleep in the morning warmth at her side, fair curly hair plastered childishly over his forehead, he saw her shake her head as if water had blocked her ears. She did not bother to wake him up so he slept on. Later, she recounted to him the dream that had woken her. In a bright, green-carpeted room she had been choosing china cups from shelves. This was a dream of anguish because of not being able to find the cups she had in mind; those she saw were too small, or too thick and heavy when she picked them up to examine them, or too large, like bowls, and she kept having to set them down in increasing dissatisfaction and disappointment because they didn't correspond to the cup she wanted.

'Was I there?' he asked, sounding silly to himself.

'You were running ahead, you kept showing me other cups,

smiling to win me over, you were producing cup-trees and con-
traptions for arranging cups conveniently and decoratively in
cupboards. But nothing would do.'

He looked at the freckles on the back of her pale, bony
hands. On one middle finger she wore a gold ring, given to her
by her father long ago; it had a small black oblong of some
stone whose name he didn't know. Her freckly face with its
small, slightly upturned nose and weak chin, seen sideways
through her mussed, wispy hair, looked oddly sewn up, like a
newly born animal to which nothing had happened yet.

This was the year that both of them, who had always been
young, would turn thirty.

All day she sat sodden in a sunny corner of the flat, saying she
must be sickening with the flu for an excuse not to have to
move, not to touch her 'work' in the other room. In the following days he left her alone. He treated her with careful
attention, as if she were really ill and couldn't cook or carry
heavy shopping.

He got people round. It was good to talk American again.
He cooked vegetarian rissoles, they listened to Springsteen
and watched TV with easy crowded sociability. She sat observ-
ing, as if she envied them. Or maybe she had had enough, he
could not tell. When his crowd left, he found himself rolling
into sleep to avoid talking to her.

'Let's get out of these rooms,' he said, not wanting to look
at her hunch up again in her corner. He pulled his lip thought-
fully. Now to his eyes the colourfulness of the apartment
emphasized some uselessness in the too fruity pattern of the
carpet. He needed to get away from her intricate sketches, the

staleness of last night's cooking, eaten in crouched discomfort at the short-legged table. Why the hell did they need so many *objects* in these two rooms, so many cushions, plants, books! In this clutter, his concentration on his film script was seeping away, soon hæmorrhaging. No longer could he listen to music, or read, especially not when she was in the flat. He would have to try taking his notebooks to l'Oiseau Bleu when she fell asleep or went out to her weekend work at the market.

They avoided the rooms and spent hours walking around the city. They wandered through the street markets with their stalls bursting with fruit, the smell of chicken and herbs, the shrunken, impoverished, venomous old women with their ugly dogs. Trailing him behind her like a bored child, she returned again and again to the window of an African import-export shop in Rue de Constance. The window, ringed by fairy lights, contained a makeshift assortment of African wigs, cosmetics, earrings, leather handbags, cowskin jackets. On the street corner at the intersection of Rue Lepic, an accordion player in dirty jeans and a long, battered pullover, like a walk-on from some Hitchcock film, and a smaller, more brazen-faced man who sang Edith Piaf songs, took to looking at them sneeringly, as if they knew they were just the sort of money-spending foreigners he and his friends could rip off if they had a chance.

'What are you after here?' he said to her, prodded to irritation by Brazen Face's scornful eyes on them.

'It gives me ideas,' she told him dreamily. 'You haven't ever been to Africa, have you? We should go to Africa.'

Up on the hill of Montmartre, under a sun-spangled blue sky, the grass on the rolling slopes of the Sacre Cœur looked springy, slippery green and, peculiarly, sheep-grazed. Did they get a flock in here at night when the gates were closed? They sat in warmth shot through with sunlight. Below them, the roofs and thoroughfares, the great train stations, the chunky spires and domes of Paris drifted in white fog. The sunlight dazzled their eyes, their hands and faces looked flabby and lifeless. In a patch of heat beside a curlicued lamp-post, a park attendant waited, motionless, nothing to do but wear his military cap and uniform. A tall African sloped past, waiting for the *gardien* to move before he unrolled his display of leather and traditional carvings for the tourists climbing the stairs of the *Butte*.

'I used to wonder how they survived, those blokes with their rolls of postcards and leather bags for sale,' she said. 'You never see anybody buy anything.'

He stretched out on the bench with his head in her lap. She scratched his scalp, her fingernails rasping, gently. An Irish guy passing said, 'Look at him, he's dead.' Sunshine penetrated their clothes. Hours later he could smell it on his skin.

What was the Paris of those young Japanese girls tripping past, trendily lipsticked, miniskirted? On the esplanade above, another pair leaned over, photographing their friends. A crowd of Chinese unloaded from a tourist bus, dressed grotesquely in loud colours, fifties-style—kneeboots, pink jackets, tam o'shanter caps on uncomfortable, fattish bodies. The time-warped style must mean they were from the People's Republic. *Nomenklatura* with papers to travel? Every one of them appeared happy, talkative. Above his closed eyes she sighed, pulling his fair hair absentmindedly through her fingers, like a peasant woman's abstracted fingering some unspun wool for its quality.

She was saying, 'The thing is, I need colour, more colour than this. The Mediterranean. Tuscany. Sunflowers whirling into the eyes. That way I'll see people in a different light, d'you know what I mean?'

She started to paint the cup dream and it turned into pile of black blockish heads on a dark-blue background. She didn't know what she would do with these heads.

The spring weather retreated again, as it always did in this city, to brownish rain. In the evenings, the rain-slicked pavements reflected tree branches like the surface of a lake. The yellow-lit brasseries and bistros were empty like stage sets. She went on talking about going away off south somewhere. He too was getting fed up with waiting for summer, with the dogshit smell that came off the streets between showers, and the hard look on the faces of overdressed, bejewelled women in leather and high shoes and fur coats with thick makeup over their winter tans, and also the brutishness of the squeeze on the metro, the German and American tourist girls laughing and giggling in the press of the unaccustomed crowd. Coming home through the rush hour, clinging to the handstraps and breathing into the sweat and ironed linen smell of a business-woman's jacket, he saw a Pakistani man, his face squashed by the crowd up against the window. On closer observation this man, in the usual cheap trousers, leather jacket and thin moustache, was younger than he himself was. On his lips an irrepressible shy smile kept coming and going at the shrieks of the girls he couldn't see in the crush behind him.

They would go to Morocco at the end of April. They had decided quickly, though the financial effort would be considerable. Going away from their jobs meant she would lose two weekends' pay and he eight nights' hotel work. They bickered a bit. She blamed him, for his lack of enthusiasm. He didn't say so clearly, not even to himself, but he was hankering after an empty room with a table, a bedsit where he could sit for six or seven hours every day and work on his revolutionary script. But bedsits required money too. Enough for a deposit, a telephone. They sold the Turkish kilim and the rocking chair and would take the rest of their savings for ten days in Morocco. Dimly he knew this trip was a risk. They had never gone away together before to come back into all the questions posed by a return. Were they capable of imagining a journey together that ended in coming back? And if so, back where? And how would they deal with the choices all this opened up? Still, he could see she had got happy again with the adrenalin of the approaching departure in her blood.

And then they were there in Morocco, arriving at night in the souk at Marrakech by bus from Ceuta. There were burning torches, a mouth-watering smell of frying fish from tables where men ate together in the firelight, cowled heads and djellabahs slipped along the edges of the dark. On the ground, vendors had spread carpets with pointed hobgoblin slippers and plates and rugs. She was delighted. He warmed to her again because she didn't enthuse openly or point out his cravenness; she didn't say, 'See, I was right, it's just a matter of getting enough together to move on.' In the alley leading to their hotel in the medina, a deep, subtle smell of poverty permeated the air around them, the most superficial layers of which he half-recognized in its aroma of unwashed clothes and aggressive crowdedness like the classrooms in Peru. Here in Marrakech, in the smell of long-preserved meat, open drains, animals, sweetness might float in the scent of cooking bread, jasmin oil, crushed mint, but the air was a palimpsest of human and animal urine, spit, sputum, old blood from the halal abbatoirs and ground-up cigarettes the rain wouldn't ever wash away.

They drank narrow glasses of tea, stuffed with sugar and mint leaves, from a stand. She bought wheels of unleavened bread from a man they met in the hotel who said he was a cook and that the bread was from a delivery for the next morning's breakfast, although the thin stretched bread rounds were so hard they must have been from the morning of that day they were still living, whose beginnings were now lost so very far away in a dream of Paris and of walking quietly down the polished staircase through the coffee scent to the first metro. In their hotel room of peeling, garish turquoise paint (she had read the colour was to ward off mosquitoes), the strangeness worked its effect. Too excited to sleep and filled with gratitude, they caressed each other to a conclusion limited for him by repugnance aroused by the stained bedsheets. Also, because they could not get the rusty tap of the shower to increase the drip from its overhead nozzle, she had washed herself from a length of hosing attached to a small tap in the communal toilet which she thought was another shower until he pointed out most Moroccans did not use toilet paper. She ridiculed his fastidiousness.

'You're the one who's supposed to be attuned to all this stuff, after all those vaunted South American odysseys ...'

'You're deluding yourself if you think you're not conditioned into your own set of fears and disgusts,' he told her, doubly irritated because he too had expected more of himself. 'It's just that you're still not come up against 'em. Just wait.'

But early the next morning, he was the one to come up against himself in the windowless toilet room where she had hosed herself down and where he willingly bore the stink to crouch over the toilet hole until a series of long cramps divested his stomach of all he had put into it in the past hours, even days, months. Then like any Moroccan, he even used the end of hosing to wash himself off, for they hadn't thought to bring toilet paper. He walked hollowly back to the room where she slept like a baby in the first light and a deep smell of old dust.

'It musta been the tea, maybe those mint leaves weren't washed. Or the fucking goat's cheese,' he told her, weak and wrathful, when she opened her eyes and sat up on her elbow, blinking puzzledly at him seated at the open window of their room over the souk. Like a child, he sat hugging the back of a wooden chair from which the paint was peeling. She considered him and tutted.

'Right. Stay here all morning and sleep. No smokes, no tea. I'll go out and buy water.' He nodded, alarmed to feel tears pricking his eyes; he felt that weak. She dressed and went out alone, to be importuned, he knew, by young men who wanted to sell to her, or buy her, or take her home. Would she know enough not to go wandering off too far alone into the medina? He stood up to go out after her, but his stomach was like a clenched fist and he lay down again quickly at the thought of that horse and donkey dust getting into his nose and lungs, put his jacket over the pillow and fell deeply asleep for, he supposed, half a day.

Intense yellow sunlight filtered through the shutters; it could only be late afternoon. On the bedside table stood a bottle of Evian. In the sun-striated dim he made her out, she was sitting watching him on the chipped chair. Briefly this moment of waking drifted to tenderness, this quiet vigilance of hers recalled those childhood afternoons of being spoiled for some childish ill in his boy's bedroom back in Chattanooga. But there was something teacherly, judgmental in her posture on the chair, her legs crossed, hands on her lap. He was glad to see she was wearing her long gypsy skirt, not her shorts, but stopped himself in the nick of time from saying so.

'We have a balcony, did you see?' she said. She got up, opened back the long windows from which flakes of dusty paint fell, heaved the peeling shutters and stepped out. He forced himself up and drank some Evian, and they sat out on the balcony, she leaning with closed eyes back into the breeze she imagined came from the desert. The sun burned whitely in a pale blue sky. They willed themselves again into the happiness of the previous night's arrival. Yet when he stood up, his head spun and he had to go again and free out his watery cramps in the toilet. He didn't understand. What had he eaten? Was this bilharzia from mint tea? After he came back to the room, she pulled the shutters to, and then closed the balcony window, saying that her arms stung with the beginnings of sunburn. He got out his notebooks and pen but it was no use; he would have to spend the rest of the day flat on his back. She left him again and went out to get something to eat. He knew that very quietly in her depths, like demonic, biblical voices of sedition in this oddly biblical country, her discontent was muttering against him for lying there with his eyes closed now of all times, wasting away their carefully plotted ten days.

This time back from the souk she had a story to tell.

Venturing into the medina in search of the hammam, she had accepted as a guide, from the usual four or five men and boys offering their services or their company, a youngish, English-speaking man with no front teeth. 'Well if it's not him it'll be someone else,' she said to herself. 'At least he speaks English.' Her mistake was feeling safer because his ugly, scarred toothlessness made her think he wouldn't dare much. He led her past the cinnamon-coloured city walls to the women's hammam, but once there she had to refuse to agree to come back to his house later and he began cursing her and gesticulating savagely. She turned away, he spat sideways and swore he would wait for her around the town with a knife, 'Fuck you, fuck you, bitch, fuck you, *putain, putain,* I cut your face,' he made the gesture on his own cheeks, fuck you, fuck you, fuck you. From this rain of hate she retreated dazed, stumbling against an old woman standing outside a nearby stall. This was a solid, rotund woman with enormous hips and waist draped in ankle-length hooded cloth like a nightdress of cheap, shimmering orange and blue cloth. As it was a woman, she looked up for succour, but the face—pale and wrinkled and marked with black henna, a long blue-black line from her mouth to her chin, small dotted diamonds at the corners of her eyes—the face incarnated indifference itself, this bulky grandmother with an expression hard and decorated like a harlot's mask, who had paused to watch the scene between the young man and the foreign, naked-haired tourist, with, in her black-ringed eyes, a look of vulgar and bored disgust.

'A real harridan, you should have seen the disappointment on her face!' She was overexcited, febrile in the telling of the story. The incident had shaken her. He wondered if she had cried, stumbling along the alleyways of stalls in the medina, ignoring the interested remarks and sex propositions of the stall-keepers trying to take her elbow and lead her into their dark shelves of goods.

'She was so bored because the scene hadn't been played out to the end, he hadn't knifed me then and there.'

'She was probably just indifferent at seeing something that in all probability happens every day in that souk.'

'Huh, I'll get myself a meat cleaver and show it to the next person that dares.'

'Well, you can't, because we're leaving this town tomorrow.'

He still felt yellowish but he wasn't going to trust to the toothless guide's being too chicken to wait for her somewhere around the hotel.

'Hell, we're not characters in a Paul Bowles story, I'm not about to leave my skin in this country.'

They caught the bus to Fez. He was pale and weak, she had absorbed some of his silence. They spent a day followed by children making ring gestures on the fingers of their left hand to ask if they were married, children offering to sell them hashish, '*chocolati! chocolati!*', and begging for pens—'*stylo! stylo!*'—for themselves, and for other brothers and sisters at home. Again there was the souk, inlaid tables and beaten copper pots and pans, leather thonged drums and other carved, embroidered items of third-world treasure—dust-gathering curios in a Western home. In the tanneries of Fez, they joined a group of Germans who were holding white handkerchiefs to their noses; this they both refused to do out of respect for the workers, though the stench turned them pale with nausea. They watched bloodsoaked hides soaking in pools of yet more blood in the concave hollows of flat roofs. From pool to pool, the half-naked workers leapt agilely under a sweaty sky.

The following morning, tired out, they settled for a few hours' smoking and watching people in a café near the bus station. They might have been in l'Oiseau Bleu, except for the big, stained, slowly rotating ceiling fan, plus the fact that they were drinking tea instead of beer and didn't dare eat any of the cakes overrun with rancid honey displayed in a plastic box on the counter. Except too for the intervention in their tête-à-tête, at separate intervals, by three men they didn't know.

They were all addressed to him, the men's words, although their eyes flicked back and forth to her and to her hands with a particular smile and insistence the travellers understood only later, on remembering that their guidebook had recommended buying curtain rings to wear as wedding bands. The first man, a thin, priestly figure in skullcap and djellabah (they all looked like professional clerics in their clothes), with a bony, nut-brown face and greeny-blue eyes, dismissed by the second as 'Ber-ber mountain people, very poor', spoke too little English or French to get further than whispery sleeve tugging. The second, a fat moustacho in western clothes under his djellabah, nodded at the clouded plastic box on the counter and wanted to buy her cakes and tea.

'You married?' he nodded, making the ring gesture on the fourth finger of his pudgy left hand.

'Euh, no. Yes. Soon. This year. Engaged.' He smiled, and to fend off the other's proprietorial attitude he also, absurdly, made the ring movement round his finger and heard her laugh.

'Ahh!' the moustacho raised his eyebrows and considered her approvingly. To him he said, 'Good! Is good? No?'

'Yeah, you dirty-minded little prick,' she said smiling, much to his alarm; did she want him to be beaten to a pulp and thrown to the big, stained wings of the fan revolving slowly over their heads? But moustacho smiled and signalled to number three, his 'friend' at another table, a young man, 'student at university, very good'. With this third in a striped woollen robe they were able to converse, even if the smooth hairlessness of his face, oddly exaggerated by a fair sparse growth on the upper lip, made him a precocious university student at fourteen or fifteen. His manner, though interested, was noticeably cooler, more neutral, interspersed with diffident glances at her hands and face. He had that look of the rough guys you see on urban transport in, say, Chicago or New York. The look that meant, *Hey you, you owe me, what you got there you took from me.* Or perhaps the student's smaller, weaker physique made it easier to express the aggression he felt. What did they do for a job in France? Teachers of English, they said. Moustacho then spread his hands and cheerily, not looking at her, invited everyone to his house. Their thanking him and having to catch a bus to Rabat was translated through the student, who then added, coolly, 'Give me your address in America, I can visit you some day.'

From his robe he produced a scrap of paper and went to the counter to borrow a pen. Watched by the three of them, moustacho, the student and her, he accepted the pen from the bar and hovered ineptly over the paper.

'Improvise, dopey,' she said to him, *sotto voce*. On the spur of the moment, unable to make up a street name, he wrote out the Boston address of a friend with whom he had been to film school and folded the paper quickly. The young man accepted it without thanks.

'You come to Morocco to teach English. Morocco need teachers.'

They went in a tourist taxi to domed villages painted turquoise and white around Fez. The weather had changed to the featureless sky that they associated with Paris. In this dull lightlessness, the poverty of the villages with their tiny, round-roofed dwellings, the dark interiors in which old men and children were practising medieval trades, weaving carpets, hammering metal in showers of sparks, cooking pottery in kilns, then the open drains, the bunches of chopped-off goat legs tied for sale in one alleyway corner, the choking, mothy dust given off by donkeys pressing through passageways and up beaten earth tracks, the ever-present flies—all this became more unbearable than either would admit. Surely such misery was but a queasy mirage? 'Just the sorta reaction that makes these set-ups go on and on,' he admonished himself. But it was no good, he couldn't take it now, he'd have to come back again, later. Alone. Better prepared. For now the hopelessness of these villages got under their skin. They bussed back to Rabat through fields of poppies and scrub dotted with palm trees, stopping off at a village to use the public toilets in the mosque. The unquestioning ease with which she covered her head with a scarf and pulled down her sleeves to enter the mosque annoyed him. Didn't she make the connection between these hidebound vestimentary rules and fat moustacho's appraising grin? He got out his notebooks again. For his character, the English teacher Anna in revolutionary Latin America, he wrote a sentence he remembered from his Chilean girlfriend: 'I would take liberty from any hand as a hungry man would snatch at a piece of bread.' Impressive in an epigrammatic sort of way. On the other hand, as always when a relationship was burning itself out, he resigned himself to the truth that he did not understand women. He could never expect to understand fully where exactly the words in their mouths were coming from. So, forgoing the young Meryl Streep, he changed his character Anna to Tom. (The younger Liam Neeson?) When they got to Rabat, he refused to smoke hashish with her in a dingy café adjoining their hotel but didn't dare to leave her alone in the café and do as he yearned, which was go up to their room alone and sit down over his notebooks.

These were the last days. Now they were more or less looking the trip back to Paris in the face. He couldn't envisage their living again after Morocco in the two attic rooms near the quartier St Paul and the bridge at Sully Morland. It annoyed him that she, who he knew saw no further than he could, would do nothing to discuss this impasse in which they were bound together, unwilling to stay put, incapable of moving forward. He was more and more restless, itchy, was continually jumping up from the table where they were sitting, or walking on ahead, staying awake longer, snatching minutes of solitude here and there with his notebooks, and at the same time stifled, tired out by the constant wariness, by her need in this country for his protection, his male presence, a need she did not always perceive. It was as if everywhere he turned, she threw up walls, invisible walls on his freedom.

Then one morning sitting on the bed pushing clothes into her backpack, she said, carefully, 'I may stay on a bit here. Go on to Tunisia. Algeria. While I'm here I'd like to see Senegal too.'

He gave a short, derisive laugh. 'What, on your own? Are you serious?'

'There's a notice downstairs looking for a fifth to share a jeep south,' she said, still pushing for space in her backpack. 'I already talked to them. They're three Germans, biologists, and one Dutch.'

'Dutch?' he repeated.

'A hophead. A Dutch hophead called Wim. Having a ball on the *chocolati*. He showed me a football of the stuff.' She grinned, her adrenalin was up at the thought of this, these new departures, unknowns. So she wasn't asking him to come along too. If she did, they would have to wait, maybe miss the jeep; his US passport would take some sorting out for these countries. There was no beating a Euro passport these days, the Euros had their special Front Doors into all these old colonies, while US citizens, despite all the tax his parents paid out to those world-capital-shifting arms deals, were still queuing at the tradesmen's entrances. He didn't ask anything else. If the Germans, for example, were male or female. He half-hoped male. Four nordic women and an Amsterdam druggie in a jeep did not augur well for their reaching any destination in Africa, no matter how many curtain rings they wore. But then perhaps none of them were set on arriving anywhere at all.

She was saying, 'They're heading for the Sahara next week.

It's so important to see the desert. I mean getting this far into Africa, without going into the desert ...' She let the unfinished sentence speak her disdain.

'Is like Paris without the *tour Eiffel*,' he said, to annoy her. 'Go for it. Painters need the desert.' Then she looked upset, she wanted him to hold her back too. He cleared his throat, it having suddenly occurred to him that this was most obviously a moment for that line from Casablanca, 'Never mind, kid. We'll always have Paris!' She laughed, he put his arm round her skinny shoulders, 'garment-hangers', he thought, his arm heavy on her jutting bones. '*Eh oui, Paris sera toujours Paris.*' In a rise of that tenderness of their first night, at the party near Bastille, he thought, panicking, that he was going to leave her alone in Africa, just as he had been left behind in Chile.

For their last two days, they left Rabat and found a hotel in a seaside village heavily polluted by the passage of diesel engines and motorbikes, but not far inland from big, molar-shaped, dark red rocks where clean breakers smashed along an unspoiled beach. At the hotel, they were told sourly that Europeans swimming or sunning on that beach risked stoning. So they walked the shoreline, skirting the rotting rubbish dumps where flies pullulated in the crevices of the dark red rocks. Instead of prospecting in town for cleaner-looking traditional restaurants – he was sick of asking for vegetarian couscous and then tasting in the vegetables the fragments of lamb from the slabs they had simply lifted out of the sauce – they made sandwiches themselves in the hotel.

It was here at this seaside town that her second story happened, as she told it to him later on that last afternoon together.

She woke early, with the first muezzin. Unable to go back to sleep in the muggy air of their room—they'd had to close the windows and shutters against mosquitoes—she got up, opened the window and leaned out in the morning air. The sky was white as November in Paris, but from the earthen street rose a hint of freshness, unpolluted by the day's diesel traffic. She got dressed, left their room, walked out of the hotel and followed the road into town, taking the opposite direction from that they had explored the day before. She always avoided taking the same way twice.

A few wizened old men on bicycles passed, then a sleepy group of younger youths on their way to work, maybe in the fields or the souk. For once, they paid her no attention; she felt cloaked in dreamlike invulnerability, except for a nagging impression of being watched from behind. Someone's eyes were on her back. During the night rain had fallen. Now the drying earth released a repellent smell of damp, petrol-stained rubbish and rotten fruit crushed or trodden underfoot from the farmers' carts that had passed in the first light on their way into town. Nearing the town, she stopped to look back at the road she had taken, at the hotel where he was still fast asleep. As if at a signal, an old, scarved woman some distance behind quickened her pace. Remembering the hard black pebble eyes of the grandmother she had jostled in the medina at Marrakech, she turned back and, not to elicit any uncalled-for attention, walked on quickly up a hill of small houses.

At that point it began to rain again. Thick, soft drops spattered the reddish, stony earth like rotten fruit thrown by children. She put down her head and hurried on in earnest, then began to run to make it to a covered marketplace she thought she had seen earlier when their bus from Rabat first pulled into town. Instead of a marketplace she entered a sort of square with alcoved walls, rather like a cloister. In the middle were rough metal frameworks that might have been some kind of penning system for animals. The place was deserted. She remembered just then that it was Friday, a holy day—that explained the peaceful, not to say lifeless air about the town. Only the itinerant merchants would work today, Berbers selling water, or the young boys on the tea and cigarette barrows, or behind their oranges arranged in pyramids for immediate squeezing.

It was raining so hard she didn't hear the footsteps of the woman behind her. She had put her hand over her mouth and nose to stop the pungent smell of animal skin raised by the rain, and then she felt someone tug the material of her gypsy skirt. She turned, not surprised to see that the woman crouching behind her was of course the scarved figure who had started up when she looked back down the road earlier. Close up, the woman was not the bent, bundled-up crone she had appeared from a distance—not a bad tactic for solitary walks in Morocco. The face held forward to her own was smooth, pretty, the skin girlish, though the black eyes, black-ringed like all women's eyes in this country, had a hard, commercial expression beyond her age. The hair and skin were undyed, unmarked with henna. At first it wasn't clear what this woman was offering or beseeching in a mixture of Arabic and French, '*Prennez-le, prennez-le madame! Il est pour vous!*' and a wrapped bundle was pushed forward.

'No, I haven't got any money to give.' She shrugged her shoulders for emphasis, '*pas d'argent, sans un sou*', then she caught sight of the small human head of surprisingly fair hair, could not believe what she imagined, and put out her hand to touch. At once the woman seized her fingers and drew them down hard on the tightly swaddled body.

'*Pour vous, pour vous, madame!*'

She looked at the blotchy face. The baby was sleeping, deeply. She had no idea if it was only a few weeks or several months old. The skin around its nose and faint eyebrows was reddish, chapped. Did that mean it had been crying? Those puffy, closed eyes struck her afterwards as a hint of character surely unusual in such a young being. Instead of a baby demand for a display of tenderness, those marks of irritation overcome by sleep signalled a sort of human camaraderie in pain.

'*Non, pas d'argent, je ne vous demande pas d'argent, madame.*'

The nearest word she had for the young woman's face close to hers was hunger. The other woman was watching her avidly, and also with some emotionlessness beyond good or evil that she had absolutely no means of reading.

'No, no.' She straightened up abruptly. 'No. *Pas question.*' Her voice sounded brittle, cruel, although she was not the one trying to hand her baby over to a stranger. In this country they all saw her as capable, indeed morally obligated to do something for them. Perhaps they were right. She looked with difficulty into the young woman's hard, shiny eyes which she had no means of reading.

She did not doubt the other woman was the mother.

'*Mais, pourquoi?*'

'*Trop!*' said the woman, holding up four fingers. '*J'en ai déjà quatre.*'

The black eyes sparked.

'*Quatre!*' she exclaimed, interested now in the implications of the situation. Later, when she recounted this exchange, he

could picture exactly that expression of readiness to be interested on her face.

But the woman had straightened up, tucked the sleeping
baby back into the material above her skirt.

'Il est si joli,' she remarked of the tight bundle. It was true;
she would not forget the expression of irritation overcome on
that sleeping face. The other woman ignored these words, she
was busy looking round at the downpour thudding less violently on the metal frames of the animal pens. Then she made
a derogatory sound in the direction of the rain, turned, and
without once looking round walked back the way she had
come, slow and bent, cronelike in the rain.

He was awake and waiting for her when she got back to the
hotel room. In one glance at each other's face, they saw that
the seditious voices of resentment setting them against one
another had disappeared. All day it rained. There was no point
in going out. Morocco was over. They lay on the bed smoking
and talking. She told him about the young black-eyed woman
who already had four children and the surprising evidence of
character in the face of the sleeping baby. Maybe this was their
last afternoon together; they spent all of it in the hotel room.
He woke up again and put the question to her: In the days to
come, when he was gone back to Paris, would she be preoccu-
pied by that woman and the sleeping baby?

'Probably not. No, the refusal was gut reflex,' she said as she
fell asleep again.

He found these words of hers out of place and lay thinking
about them until, irritably, he decided they told him nothing
he didn't already know about her character. Then, sleepless in

the sound of the rain, his cheek on her wispy hair, he wondered how he would have reacted if she had brought the baby back to the hotel with her, if it were lying sleeping beside them, its eyes and mouth closed like hers in sleep, three soundless, tightly drawn lines.

the marriage
at antibes

'Oh, we are going to be so happy away from the things that
almost got us but couldn't because we were too smart for them!'
—ZELDA FITZGERALD, *Save Me the Waltz*

'Their sea here is not a real sea, did you know? It's nearly surrounded by land, like our Caspian,' Khosro informed Nasima, drawing yet another comparison between France and back home. She wanted to say, *Why are you trying to teach me about a place I've just left and where you haven't been for more than ten years?* But the tone of these words would be her brother Bahram's, a trader's voice, picking at the merchandise offered him for sale. Nasima, they always said, 'wouldn't hurt a fly'. The middle sister of five brothers, she had always known how to bide her time, unbothered, uncomplaining, fond. She desired, she said when the girls she had gone to school with came visiting, to look after someone, to care for another person … Their giggles cut her off, in their excited voices they called out (Bahram working with the uncles in another room heard them), 'Oh, Nasima's going to get married soon!' Occasionally, that last year, at a marriage or a farewell meal for someone parting on a pilgrimage south or to visit family in Europe, Nasima found herself crying more than was called for, along with the mother and sisters of the host family. Her mother said, 'You're no longer a child, these tears of loss are not a child's tears,' her words as usual smoothing away possible questions, restoring faith. And the seasons had come round, events had taken their course and now here she was, at the end of the first year of her marriage to Khosro, standing in a street in the south of France, stooping over her baby Taghi in his pram.

'Look at the sea! What does the sea say? Whoosh, whoosh!'

She pointed out to him, between palm trees and hotels, Khosro's unreal sea. The Mediterranean really did look like a child's painted sea this afternoon, a saucer of blue varnish under a benign sky. Below the ancient ramparts, the narrow beach (its pale, naked bodies haphazardly scattered) remained hidden from view. Once, in the heat of a weekday afternoon when Khosro was working, Nasima had ventured through the undressed crowd, dragging the pram over the sand as far as the first wavelets, where she crouched, prickly with embarrass-ment, restricting her gaze to the motionless horizon that did not churn with naked European limbs. At home, women bathed fully dressed, skirts and long blouses billowing and unbalancing them heavily in the shallows. Nasima did not know how to swim. That evening in their hotel, laughing, half avoiding Khosro's eye, she described to him her conviction that on the beach as many people were looking and commenting on the prudishness of her cotton dress as at home they would have hissed their hate had she dared to sit thus among a crowd, bare-legged, bare-armed and without a headscarf. Khosro folded his lips and looked at her seriously, possibly annoyed or afraid at her imprudence.

'It's too soon,' he said. 'You're trying these things too *quickly*. You have to wait a while.' Her humour dampened, she watched his face until he got up and stood at the window with his back to her, looking down on the sea, on the white yachts massed placidly and sparkling in Port Vauban, inside the harbour walls of Old Antibes. Taghi, placed carefully on his left side in his cot, was sleeping what Khosro called his 'amphibious sleep, little arms stretched one over the other like gills'.

Khosro was not relaxed. Three hours after his return to the hotel room, he had not changed out of the dark trousers and shirt he wore to the laboratory, and this despite her leaving out his home pyjamas and slippers for him to pull on as soon as he came in the door. Leaning at the window with his back to her, he talked perhaps to himself, perhaps to Nasima watching from the bed.

'Flat as a stagnant pond, hard to believe it's not dead, this Mediterranean. But it renews itself from Atlantic streams around Gibraltar, more or less once every two thousand seven hundred years.'

Grinning, he turned round, 'For Europeans two thousand years is sacred! The beginning of time. Our peasants drink out of wells twice that age without knowing what they are doing!'

Now it was Nasima's turn not to join in. Calm and bemused from the side of the bed where she kept her vigil over the baby's cot, she pondered his words. Here, exactly, was what she didn't understand in Khosro. She had prepared herself to find a man with the habits and attitudes of another country. In many ways Khosro, who had lived in Paris for the past ten years, was as 'occidentalized' as her brother Bahram had warned. To Nasima's ears, there was even an awkward turn of phrase, a foreign lilt to his speech. Though of course, what did she know? Apart from pilgrimages south and short visits to their capital, Nasima herself had never travelled before marriage brought her to France. But—this was it—in Khosro's opinions the expressions 'European', 'Western', kept turning up, as they did in the television and newspapers back home. Nasima was just beginning to understand that Khosro still referred to himself mentally as a man from their country, and that by this last word he meant the provincial town in the northern plain where they had both grown up, as distinct from what he called the 'hotchpotch' of their capital. In the first days after Taghi's birth in Paris, there had been a dull surprise she did not have time to think about on hearing in Khosro's mouth the words of their dialect when he picked Taghi up, 'little devil, my little *shaytoun, batchéyé bâzigoush*'.

What did you expect, she could hear Bahram sneer, *that he had lost the use of his own mother tongue?*

No. Yet … when the marriage talks began, a year previously, Nasima had imagined Khosro's years in France, his diplomas from European universities, making any child of theirs different. Different, from the very first breath it drew, from all the other babies born back home.

Every morning, feathery clouds floated on the snow-striped flanks of the Alps that made a semi-circle around Antibes. Khosro had found research work in the new science park inland. For the first few months they lived in a hotel. Khosro was working too hard to go flat-hunting, and Nasima still hadn't mastered enough French to negotiate with estate agents. She walked the pushchair through the town, admiring people's clothes, the pale pink and pastel green of the old town houses, the gleaming tinted glass balcony fronts of the luxury flats. These clean, edible colours were more like the Europe she had imagined than the stained, roaring boulevards of northern Paris where for the first months she had shared Khosro's life in a shoebox *chambre de bonne*. She definitely preferred these toy-like, cobbled alleyways smelling of cooking *provençale* to the crowded streets around the room where Khosro and his books had been living up seven flights of stairs under the eaves for all of his unmarried life. On the long trek with the pushchair to the hypermarket out of town (Khosro told her to avoid the overpriced olive barrels and fruit of the *marché provençale* in Old Antibes), Nasima delighted in picturing the glamorous, high-ceilinged interiors of the villas she passed. She must put pressure on Khosro to make an effort and find them a flat. Living in a hotel you were still on the outside. Nasima retained her country's suspicion and pity for hotels as emblems of unattachment and lawlessness. She was impatient to be inside, to belong. She hadn't told her family they were still in a hotel, she had only repeated how very pleased with Khosro she was for bringing her here. To her unmarried cousins she wrote letters describing how people of all ages in the streets were decked out as for a wedding. She had even seen a leathery-skinned old woman in tight, white shorts and a fringed sleeveless top walking a poodle in the warm sunshine, a woman the age of their grandmother's sister Aziza. In their home town, women of that age moved weakly and breathlessly in their burdens of watery flesh, the accretion of years of cooking and childbearing. Aziza had scarcely left home since her husband's death. And how the neat edges of low-walled gardens and ornamental gates, the parasolled terrasses around old fountains, reminded her of the rich area inhabited by Europeans and government ministers in the north of their capital! Nasima expressed her contentment to Khosro. He said easily, 'Oh yes, these suburbs are as international as multinational companies,' then, unsmiling, pulled her to him to walk with his arm round her shoulders. Nasima was still unfamiliar enough with this gesture in public for it to keep her quiet. Khosro, looking down at his baby son's bald head, murmured, 'This is like a dream being with you two here.'

The apartment block they were to visit had been described as 'recent'. Khosro said this meant built in the last twenty to thirty years. 'Before the recession, there was enough money in Europe for governments to promise everyone a house, never mind the quality.' Nasima wasn't listening. Now that they were to begin to belong to their lives here, she could only concentrate on her own excitement. As in the days of getting ready for marriage in France, she was mesmerized by the passage through the mirror into another mode of being, half glimpsed and pored over since girlhood: married life and the world outside their own country, the lands where their newspapers said all beliefs and values were lived in reverse and turned upside down.

But that afternoon, their first minutes on the inside of pretty Antibes proved disappointing. The stairs and hallway of this apartment building, done over with clean and ugly square tiles like a hospital, smelt of stale cooking. 'Cabbage,' Khosro said, in their own language. The estate agent made a comment as if in explanation. Khosro translated, 'There are a lot of retired people in these cheaper apartments.' *Old people's cooking, soft diets*, thought Nasima, faintly disgusted. Her large, oval face retained its outward placidity, for she never put herself

forward by complaining. The presence of strangers accentuated her natural deference. She kept lowering her eyes, and
touching her long, naked hair lightly, embarrassed for the
estate agent by the wide stare she directed at Nasima and then
at Khosro and back again at Nasima and the baby, trying to
connect all three. She was old, this woman, her hair too vivid
blonde for her skin. Mascara muddied her short eyelashes, the
old blue of her eyes had the brittle shine of nail polish though
the eyes were watery, spilling over their stubby thickened
lashes like overripe fruit. A fruit preserved too long in honey
and sugar and leaking into the sweetness around it ... Just after
her arrival, keys in hand as if she had not a minute to spare,
Khosro had appeared, dapper and harried in the dark jacket
and trousers he wore to work. His manner as he introduced
himself and Nasima was graceful. 'Royal,' Nasima said to herself again, with a little flush of pride, that word she was careful never to say aloud. Royal was associated with the régime so
hated by the political movement her brothers had started calling 'Khosro's people'. With the estate agent, Khosro smiled a
lot. His movements were keen and energetic. Perhaps without
Nasima, for whom Khosro had to translate everything, the
other woman would have thought Khosro, pale from overwork
and with his polished Parisian accent, his suit and briefcase,
came from some other town in France. Khosro knew how to
take the conversation where he wanted, unlike Nasima, who
stood back shyly, watching for appropriate moments to smile.
In the dark under Khosro's eyes, Nasima detected his fatigue.
He met her eyes only fleetingly, reserving his warmth for
Taghi whom he hadn't seen all day, as he helped Nasima with
the pushchair up a short flight of stairs into a lift, stood aside,
held open the doors and found a light switch, touching

Nasima on the back and shoulder to urge her before him or make her stand back for the estate agent. Nasima pressed Taghi's head lightly to check his warmth and again felt the other woman's eyes on her long manicured nails and the black curtain of hair that kept drifting back over her face. Taghi moaned crossly. *Is he hungry already?* Nasima wondered aloud, looking at Khosro to translate, but Khosro was taking advantage of the women's interest in the baby to think of something else. She stooped, pushing back her hair. Taghi stuck out his lower lip, found his thumb and looked away. Like Nasima the baby was a peaceful being. At the moment his favourite occupation was stuffing his fingers or a toy into his mouth, filling his lungs and wailing though his stopped-up lips, but he had absorbed enough of Nasima's decorum to not ever perform thus in public. The other woman asked Khosro how old Taghi was, Nasima could understand that much. 'Four and a half months,' she said, smiling, lifting her son a little in his pushchair and adjusting the seatbelt over his trousers. The other woman's breath smelled of bad sweetness—the word for it in their language meant the wind off a stagnant river—given off by the digestion of too much rich food.

The lift doors opened. Khosro caught his son's round eyes looking up at him brightly. He caressed the baby's head and, waiting until the estate agent clicked smartly ahead in her high-heeled shoes, he bent down hungrily, too hungrily, whispering in Taghi's ear and squeezing his face against his son's soft cheek. The baby dealt with this incursion by placing his thumb in his mouth and sucking furiously, eyes glazing over until his father had retreated.

Under the electric light in the shuttered flat, the estate agent's skin possessed the same blonde powderiness as her dyed hair. She was explaining again. Khosro translated, 'Most of the flats are rented or owned by elderly people who have come to this corner of France to retire in the clement sea air. The apartment is furnished and we ask you not to displace the furniture.' Nasima stood behind the pushchair, breathing in the camphor-laden dust of great, heavy, shiny sideboards and tables that reminded her of the house of her grandmother's sister Aziza, who had rarely bothered washing herself in the years of her widowhood. As in her grandmother's sister's house, bibelots and gimmicks, clocks, calendars, straw toys, little dusty mats covered any available surface. Weighty, padded chairs surrounded a huge linoleum-covered table. The bedroom smelt of mouldy clothes. In the living-room, a heavy oak fan on the ceiling represented huge ugly flower petals with a calyx of fogged amber lampshades. A line of porcelain insects graced the kitchen wall over the stove. Nasima jumped, taking them for flies; Khosro translated crickets. The estate agent ignored the dust and the unwashed fug, the tasteless tourist artefacts, and trotted through the rooms, pulling open windows and shutters. Nasima and Khosro followed her proprietorial sweep, looking politely out of the windows as invited. Daylight filled the apartment as the shutters were folded back, revealing nicotine-coloured stains on the ceiling and tidemarks on the grey carpet. Beneath Nasima's calm, Khosro read the distaste of a good housekeeper.

'I can't take any more time off to look around,' he hissed. 'Anyway, there's no way we can afford more than this.'

The estate agent called them to the bedroom window. Below, in a little field of flattened grass turning to hay, stood an elegant, disused villa whose garden of lemon and pear trees and rose arbour growing in beautiful disarray over a ruined verandah and gateway contrasted the botched ugliness of its bricked-up windows. One corner of the verandah facing their block of flats was draped in cardboard. In the pinkening end of the afternoon, Khosro and Nasima made out a hand poised just above the edge of the cardboard and in the hand was a book. Someone had settled into a cardboard shelter beneath one of the bricked-up windows. For a minute, the reading hand absorbed in the book held the attention of the woman and the couple at the window. Over the cardboard, they made out the top of a tonsured, grey-haired head, as diffident as a head behind a newspaper on a train or some café terrasse. The estate agent reached out to close the window, commenting briskly, 'There'll be less of them now the season's over.' Khosro repeated for Nasima, his neutrality signalling her to keep any reaction to herself. 'They are not French, they come from Eastern Europe to work the tourists.' Nasima, her hand on the baby's cheek, nodded. Lifting Taghi in her arms, she followed into the kitchen where their guide was pulling at the window latch. Khosro hastened to help, leaned out, clapped back the shutters and stood back deferentially.

'*Voilà, m'sieur-dame!*' the estate agent announced, opening her hands at the view.

'*Magnifique,*' Khosro murmured. At the sound of this word she knew and liked, Nasima smiled, making Taghi look up at her face and say 'Ah!' with pleasure.

'Madame must be afraid of heights since she doesn't dare come near to see for herself!' All the old blonde teeth showed in her laugh. Khosro beckoned Nasima forward. *Not difficult to understand why she wants you to look* out *of this dump,* murmured

Bahram's voice. *Don't tell me you've come all the way to Europe to live in old Aziza's front room!* Nasima looked out the window. Below them she saw a busy road; on the other side, over a line of orange-roofed houses and a railway track where a train was pulling in slowly, its grey sides shining in the sun, there was the port, the white triangles of its moored yachts, and the picture-book Mediterranean, and further back again, the snowcaps of blue and purple mountains like the mirage of a magic land or the traceries of the mountains of paradise whose running streams and gardens she was familiar with from the illustrations of their classical poetry.

'Say something, for heaven's sake, show an interest,' Khosro pleaded irritably under his breath. In his voice she heard again the effort he was making to hold off his own fatigue. To calm him, Nasima said, '*C'est bien, c'est bien,*' but the other woman was not listening for her reaction. As far as she was concerned, the flat was a deal for Khosro 'and his young family'. She pointed out the old black-and-white television on top of a teak commode in the living-room, and detailed the functioning of the communal heating and the water mains. Without reading it, Khosro signed a dog-eared inventory from a drawer in the kitchen.

'One more thing,' said the woman, after giving Khosro the keys.

Afterwards, Khosro translated to Nasima what she then added; at the time, Nasima was standing behind Khosro, her hand lightly on his shoulder. He liked her to relax with him in front of others. Nasima was smiling her warm smile of leave-taking; she always enjoyed the moment other people went away and left them alone together with Taghi.

The estate agent no longer looked at her, she was directing

her last words to Khosro. 'There will only be the three of you, won't there? Because believe me, people in this building will soon notice if you bring in other family.'

'What did she mean?' asked Nasima, gently, puzzled. 'Other family? We don't have family here.'

'They imagine we'll have other family from home. Maybe she thinks another wife and children.' Nasima laughed out loud, but Khosro's lips were thin. She looked at him, shocked. But a moment later he had seized his son and held him in the air above his head, chanting his half-mocking singsong litany of love names the baby must now know by heart, my little son, our little son, our heart, my little heart, eyes of my life, little burnt father, little devil-god, little handsome god ... Nasima was laughing and catching Taghi's feet to tickle them, and only at the back of her mind was she thinking of how during the marriage negotiations had been quoted Khosro's grandfather's praise of Khosro's 'respectfulness in anger'. Khosro's grandfather, a canny, unsmiling septuagenarian in a white skullcap, always seated with his back to a wall, his hands placed kingly fashion, palm down on his knees, struck awe into the most hardbitten *bazaari* in their town. Coming from his mouth, this phrase about Khosro's 'respectfulness in anger' had impressed Nasima's father and carried the day. All through the marriage talks, her family had worried about the shameful associations of Khosro's being a political refugee, one of the renouncers, those who had given up on their country. But a man with respect would not make his wife violently unhappy.

That first night, Khosro got the black-and-white TV set working while Nasima bathed Taghi and settled him to sleep.

Khosro opened out a sofa-bed; they placed two of their own rough wool kilims on it to protect themselves from the dust of previous occupants and sat cross-legged, their backs to the wall. Nasima's eyes grew heavy as Khosro translated pieces of news for her. Unemployment in Europe, Parisian bus strikes, the US presidential election, a European conference on meat prices. Far south in Africa—'but not as far from here as our town', said Khosro—in a grey jungle swamp, families fled war. They stared at a baby with a big insect head, sitting on the grey ground at his mother's feet and drinking from an old petrol canister. Khosro translated on and on and his face grew greyer and his voice more expressionless. 'Don't, if you're tired,' said Nasima. He shrugged. Nearly every night since she had arrived in France, he had made a point of translating her the news. He wanted her 'to understand the place where she was living'. The national news switched to regional: pollution and its effect on schoolchildren, a referendum on banning tramps from the streets of Nice and the surrounding towns. Taghi called from his cot, Nasima got off the sofa-bed to go to him. When she came back, Khosro was curled up, fast asleep where he had been sitting. For a minute, she looked in consternation at his folded arms, his head tucked tightly into his chest as if he forbade himself to use up any more space than the bare minimum. He looked like a tramp sleeping in a doorway, though with none of the diffidence of the old man reading in his cardboard shelter outside. Nasima turned off the television, fetched some blankets and pillows and lay down wide-eyed beside Khosro, who curled tightly away from her, like a mollusc in its shell.

From as far back as she could remember, Nasima had known Khosro, as much as she knew any boy who was not her brother, from seeing him play with the others at weddings and engagement parties. There were five brothers and one sister. The father, like most men in their town, traded in the bazaar. Khosro, the middle boy, stood out in her mind for his slightness, a gracefulness in his face. There was a touch of royalty—she meant a superior apartness—about Khosro. In their town, everyone knew Khosro would have inherited a princely fortune had he not fled the country after the revolution. Even now, his grandfather hoped to leave the family lands and caravanserai to his middle grandson. The elder brothers would have the house and factory, but Khosro, had he not disappeared to France, was natural inheritor of the caravanserai that had been in the family for so long no one remembered the name of the first man to hew, haggle, or marry into possession of those lion-coloured, sand-scoured courtyards in the desert plains. As well as being his grandfather's favourite, Khosro had been renowned at home for his hard, conscientious attitude to schoolwork. The teachers (most later run out of town by Khosro's classmates for their pro-régime sympathies) used to leave him to teach the class in their absence, although they took care to appoint him the support of a heftier boy like Bahram, Nasima's brother. Khosro alone was too fine a figure to win if his authority came down to a punch-up.

Khosro's father kept songbirds and canaries. When Nasima went past their part of the walled alley between back courtyards on her way to return or borrow from neighbours, she heard Khosro's father's birds singing. Automatically she recalled Khosro's thin face, its darkness and girlish elegance. Nasima was fourteen or fifteen when the birdsong stopped.

Khosro's father had died of cancer. Now she no longer knew when she was walking past Khosro's part of the alley of high stained walls along the open drain of filthy water that ran down the alley. Later, Khosro told her that after his father's death no one had bothered to clean out the cages until such a mountain of guano accumulated that they had to set the surviving birds free.

Nasima left the windows open all day in the prismatic sunlight shining off the snowcapped Alps and the sea with its patches of jade diluted in saturated blue. She stuffed the gimmicks and ornaments into a cupboard, burned incense to get rid of the mustiness from the carcasses of ugly furniture and the stale cooking smells seeping up from the flats downstairs. Soon from the kitchen came the elusive, high scent of the *zaffron* with which she flavoured their daily rice, and the tang of the huge plastic bags of pungent dried vegetables for soup she had brought over because you couldn't find them anywhere in France.

Khosro and Nasima settled into a routine. In the first light, before the sun cleared the mountains, Taghi woke them by rattling the toys attached to his cot and floating on the air clear sounds, long, short, loud and so soft as to be imperceptible. Often in the morning the sea was milky emerald. When Taghi took his first bottle, white groundmist and clouds floated on the mountain shoulder. The summits kept their distinctness for an hour or so before fading into the white blue grey of sky and ground towards the middle of the morning.

Khosro said he was afraid Nasima would be homesick and bored, but her days slipped by with surprising facility. In the mornings she washed and cleaned and prepared meals for the three of them. In the afternoons she visited the park, the beach, the supermarket or the post office. She was happy with Taghi and his fuzzy hunger- or sleep-tinted consciousness of the world and himself, which she imagined drifting along with her over the pushchair, like the bubble cloud of thoughts over a comic-strip character's head. In the evenings Khosro and Nasima watched Taghi's every movement with pride and amazement. Khosro videoed him lying on her stomach, half rolling over and raising his heavy head. 'He's like you,' said Khosro, with immense gratitude that astonished Nasima. 'Full of goodwill.' He shook his head. She laughed him out of his sobriety until he made a face at Taghi, who was watching Nasima intently, the corners of his mouth turning up in a smile when her eyes or voice changed expression. In his hands, long-fingered like her own, Taghi now took anything they gave him, pieces of Khosro's lab papers, or newspapers, plastic toys, Nasima's hair-slides. Carefully, repeatedly, he examined each object, bringing it up to his mouth, holding it out at arm's length, turning it slowly to memorize its form. He was all that she desired. The renewal of his presence, bright-eyed in his cot every morning, reaffirmed what she had always known, ever since the days of the battered doll she fought over with the youngest of her brothers, that all her life long she had really been expecting his beauty. Her only wonder had been exactly how this gorgeousness would take form ... *Even the cockroach's mother adores her son*, Bahram teased when Nasima sent photos of Taghi along with letters detailing his movements and expressions. The only unexpectedness had been the frailty of his very fine, light hair, like the hair she saw on European babies. 'It must be the bad water here,' she wrote to her cousin.

At night she undressed Taghi for his bath, and he stretched from head to toe, then blissfully batted his arms in the air towards her, making high-pitched squeaks while she chanted, *'A-tal, ma-tal, Too-too lay / Gâv-é Hassan tche tour é'*. Sometimes she was taken aback by the knowledgeable shine in his eyes fixed on hers as he fell asleep, his evident satisfaction that she had made the best—the only—choice for both of them.

The baby Taghi was right. By luck and forbearance, holding to a sense of direction, Nasima had escaped a disastrously wrong turning. Now in this town by a warm sea, mother and baby had their first calm. As if having come a great distance, she was breathing quietly in the shelter of a tree or rock, assured that the danger once so close remained far behind. Khosro had not been the first to ask her family about Nasima's marriage plans. Soon after Nasima's twenty-fourth birthday, a rich *bazaari* from their town had begun inquiring after her. This was a man at the optimum marriageable age for men, still in his early thirties, but very hard, having acquired, in a short space of time during the war in the south, the wile and acumen of traders as seasoned as Khosro's grandfather, by dealing in the black market for food ration tickets. With a growing sense of helplessness, Nasima refused his queries. She was hoping for a teacher, or a university graduate. However, her whole family was dazzled by the *bazaari*'s wealth. Her father prevailed upon her for a meeting—'It's only polite to see him, talk to him!' Nasima sat wrapped in her veil on the far side of the room. She did not look at him, rather she kept her eyes into the shadow of herself, as if turning her face from a scalding light. Only once, in the middle of the conversation, when her father stood up and turned to accept a tray of tea from her cousin in the corridor, did Nasima raise her eyes, which instantly caught his, flicking over her like a tongue. The contact was intimate enough for her to remember afterwards how the beauty of his eyes with their long eyelashes underlined the hard suspicion, the ready derision of their expression. For days afterwards, that physical presence, the hard stomach rounding already in the thin body, the big, hooked nose and regulation heavy moustache, the flat, straight hair, left their imprint on her, as intimately as if she had spent that hour close enough to him to feel his breath on her face. Later, she found out that any type of behaviour other than her reclusive silence would have worked more to her favour, if she had pushed her veil back off her forehead and talked naturally to her father for example, for reports came back that the other man had found Nasima represented his womanly (the word in their language also meant wifely) ideal, *gifted with a tranquillity rare among unmarried girls of her age today.*

'You are too demanding. You're only making things worse,' said Bahram, though he sympathized with her fears, at least until she chose Khosro. Three years previously, their father had married Bahram into a rich butcher's family. He now spent his days in charge of the accounts at the local abbatoir.

'One day, sooner or later, you have to do like me and everybody else and make a choice. Why should you be different? Count your blessings you won't have to leave behind your country and family, like Hussein's sister Zoreh. They're doing all they can to hold off any commitment.'

Thus Nasima heard of Khosro's family's futile attempts to find him a wife willing to go to France. The problem with Khosro was not so much his living in exile as his previous political commitments. Men who had been politicized were not good providers. They gave their money to underground organizations, they risked exposing their families to police attention, not to mention disappearing for years into prison or going into hiding. They got killed, or executed. Then their wives and children became burdens for any family-in-law who would take them on.

At the weekends, Khosro walked with Nasima and Taghi around the *marché provençal* with its population of tourists' artists selling what Khosro called rubbish—coloured stones, bags of lavender, sculptures in wood and iron, overpriced beer. At half past four on the first clear winter days, all the old were out in the cafés and shops. Nasima observed their clean, matching trousers and jackets, scarves, and expensive winter coats and shoes, making a mental note of the cuts and combinations for her cousin at home who supported her husband's teaching and taxi driving with her dressmaking. Khosro saw her noticing and made scornful remarks. 'Splutocrats,' he called the pebble-eyed old men on their sticks.

'What do you mean?' she puzzled.

'Spluttering plutocrats,' said Khosro. 'They don't talk. If you ask them a question they splutter.' Over Taghi's head in the pushchair, he continued in the same vein, talking and comparing as they edged the pram slowly through the crowds.

'The charm of this town for Europeans is the Roman feel, the sense of the centuries and centuries of living off the plundered fat of the land. They admire this epicureanism in the sunlight, this unmental cult of the body.'

Nasima didn't understand his tone. She liked the pretty yellow façades and the clean cobblestoned *ruelles*. Her only wonder was that in all their vilifications of Western habits, the newspapers at home had never once mentioned that Europeans respected dogs as much as the Hindustanis were known to honour their cows. The old had dogs, the young couples had dogs, the destitute young and old sitting on the ground outside supermarkets and banks had tamed wolfhounds. Even Taghi made a friendly squeak of recognition when he saw a dog trotting past, tail in the air. By now Nasima had quelled her instinct to jump and cross the road as she would have back home, where dogs in the streets were savage and hungry and, in their religion, synonymous with everything dirty, outcast and insulting. In all his years in France, Khosro had not lost his disgust for the animal. He still turned his head and spat when they passed dog turds on the pavement.

Usually on these afternoon walks they followed the crowd down to the narrow half-moon beach, La Gravette, on the other side of the ramparts, or up to a small, chalky castle against the sky. The castle rooms were hung with the work of a real artist, Picasso, whose name Nasima had heard before, but whose paintings Khosro did not think they should have to pay money to see. Taghi giggled, then cried as his pushchair jiggled over the cobblestoned path around the ramparts abutting the *hôtel de ville*. Off the sea the wind blew with a wild salty scent. Nasima thought of Khosro's caravanserai, the sand-blown courtyards, one big and one small, and the well, hundreds of years old, which still gave water though it smelt of cold dust. In Port Vauban, yachts the size of condominiums dazzled transfiguringly white in the sunlight and wind rippling the water into the faceted surface of a turquoise jewel. Khosro talked about how their country would never be able to manufacture such luxury yachts. Who would trust enough to buy from them? Nasima admired a four-masted yacht and his sneers redoubled. How many years of the average family's income would be necessary to buy such a thing? Nasima proposed a figure, Khosro crushed her at once. Luxury is not for people who work. As if to prove his point, he recognized the yacht of a French politician on trial for bribery and corruption who had declared this and other yachts to the Inland Revenue as a storage cargo ship. Nasima, her eyes on the graceful white palace, like a mirage between water and the sky, was only half listening again. At home she had learnt the safest way to live with other people's politics was to ignore them. Thus, she had never told Khosro how in the beginning, before she had got used to him, it had startled her to hear him talk with fervour that would make people at home smile bitterly. The blood and loss of the repression following on the revolution, after the first waves of activists like Khosro had gone into exile, had rendered this language hollow forever. Hearing Khosro's words now, her brothers, her uncles, even their wives, would curl their lips saying, 'Does he think he's so pure? But he too has his price, like everyone else. It's just a question of knowing how much.' Away from Khosro, from the pushchair, and Taghi, Nasima looked up to the sky and the Alps behind the shore route to Nice. She stared at the seeming contradiction of the pale blue, sunny sky behind the snowy mountain shoulders. Now in the early winter evening, rose-coloured clouds trailed gauzily in the clear, fading blue. She had never seen such colours in the industrialized plains around their northern town … 'They look as if they've drifted off a Michelangelo fresco,' said Khosro, following her eyes, 'as if you might see cherubs cavorting, those baby angels with dimply bottoms Christians paint on the roofs of their cathedrals. Look.' He indicated the deepening blue-pink over the bay of Nice. The sea had whitened lighter than the sky. They watched for a minute in silence, interrupted by Taghi's loud, sleepy plaint, then turned back to the flat. On the other side of the town where the sun had disappeared, the sky thinned to the lightest saffron. The purple hulks of the mountains looked like extinct volcanoes, before fading magically into blue mist with a last, distant opacity on their white caps.

Every morning, Nasima saw the tramp who lived on the balcony of the overgrown villa shaving behind his sodden cardboard, then putting on a damp greatcoat and sometimes a baseball hat, and even fumbling in his pockets as if for keys. Then he left his cardboard shelter and walked down the untidy, arboured garden path to its rusty gate and letterbox.

The autumn sky was high and pigeon-coloured. By eleven o'clock, smoky leaf fires from the villa gardens scented the air heavily while Taghi slept, arms outflung in his morning nap. He could hold his bottle now by himself, making a game of pushing it away, gazing at the teat, jamming it ineptly against his lower gums. At six and half months he had filled out and was solid and strong, though sniffly in the mornings. From the very beginning, Taghi had been a round, smooth baby, dispensing happiness, never shrivelled, irate or closed-up in fœtal sleep. He was bigger than most babies she saw in town, healthy and as appetizing as the red and yellow apples in the local fruit shops ... How people looked when she took him out in the pushchair! Most women and some men, young men too, all with desire in their eyes. Nasima had never imagined that a baby, like a woman, could be the focus of desire. She dressed him in a red, white-collared matinée coat, navy tights and a blue tailed pixie hat in blue and white check. Instead of shoes, which he always kicked off, he wore yellow socks with clown faces and bells. When they were not with Khosro, the baby received a lot of admiration from the well-dressed old people and skinny, middle-aged women. Checking her face first, Taghi responded to their smiles, his thumb poised wetly, ready to suck if he needed it.

'They think you are Italian when you are not with me,' said Khosro, moodily, when she relayed to him their compliments.

'Why don't they think you are Italian too?'

'No, you don't get it. Together we don't look like a European couple.'

'Why? Because of your age?' She stared at him, her calm eyes intense, penetrating, as if in her rare anger she would like to shake his head free of its thoughts as vigorously as she had rid the flat of its dust. It angered her that he did not see the innocence of Taghi's charm. When they were out with Khosro, people smiling into the baby's face glanced up and away from Khosro's dark expression, which walled Taghi off from the rest of the world. Nevertheless, for the moment Nasima was trying to forget her husband's surliness. He was so tired. In the evening his eyelids were swollen and his eyes dry from the detailed attention necessary to his work in the laboratory. Instead of admitting to his fatigue, he said, 'So many people in this town have nothing or very little to do all day. Young mothers like you. The tourists. Tramps. The retired.' Yet, no matter how she asked, he would not stop work for a few days. 'I'm not used to taking holidays,' he said, perhaps reminding her obliquely that unlike her own brothers, who had always lived off their family, Khosro had worked for a living since losing his father at the age of fourteen. During his time at the *lycée* in their town, he used to get up at four o'clock to go to the bakery warehouse and bring back boxes of glazed, gluey caramel fingers to sell in the afternoons. Nasima herself had eaten them on the way home from school, cakes called *bahmiyyeh* which afterwards required several cups of tea to clean the gluey sweetness from the teeth.

Today Khosro was part of a European team in rivalry with an American laboratory. He could not afford to let up. Also, he had only been in this job for little more four months, since their arrival in the south of France, and he did not want to give his employers the impression he was finding the pace too tiring.

But then, events finally forced Khosro to stay at home from work. A great statesman had died. All shops and companies would close for a day of national mourning. In Paris, long funeral ceremonies were planned. Nasima was happy. Official mourning in France did not, as in their country, entail the interdiction to go out, or to be seen laughing or eating in the street. They could take the train somewhere for a day, maybe up to the mountains whose hypnotic beauty came and went from their windows. She might make a picnic for an afternoon on the Nice seafront. Early that holiday morning, however, Khosro turned on the television commentary on the funeral proceedings in Paris. The screen showed the statesman's coffin, waiting in the empty centre of a great square ringed by a military orchestra, opposite the massive open doors of the Pantheon. Nasima shivered. 'Let's go out,' she urged, her voice to herself sounding like a plea. 'Like a birth in reverse,' said Khosro unexpectedly, incomprehensibly. She waited, but he sipped his tea, mesmerized and bitter, adding his own counterpoint to the presenter's respectfully muted observations on the glory of the Pantheon.

'Unbelievable! The need to *frenchify* heaven! An extraordinary lay canonization! Like all quasi-religio-political ceremonies, doubly empty because the power of the symbolism has gone. We are out of that age where it worked, in 1764 when whoever it was commissioned the construction of the Pantheon. A great, primitive denial.'

The president appeared on the steps of the open mausoleum wearing a greatcoat, his nose red in the cold rain. An army orchestra struck up. 'Christ's prayer in Gethsemane,' said the voice-over. Khosro added derisively, 'Marie Curie is the only woman in there, you know!' He shook his head. 'Ha! This is the society that claims equality for women.'

Nasima turned away, she was superstitious about death. She gathered up Taghi, who was moaning bad-temperedly. He had picked up her sense of expectation for this day with Khosro at home. 'Let's go to the beach,' she said brightly to him, pre-empting his screech for attention. They left Khosro cross-legged in his pyjamas over his glass of tea, opposite the TV screen with its coffin on trestles in a great rain-swept Parisian square ...

The sea, usually so benign, was eerily flecked, lit from within under a solid sky. Nasima took the route to La Gravette. There too the spoon-shaped tongue of water was in activity, and the little semicircle of sand empty but for two kids flying vampire-shaped kites whose cracking dives Taghi took his thumb out of his mouth to watch interestedly. The usual tourists had deserted the cobbled streets along the ramparts, the restaurants had their green boards up. Down from Picasso's castle wind blew so hard that Nasima finally turned back, past the railway station where covered goods trains waited for the holiday to be over. All this would be so heavy if it wasn't for

Nasima's chanting aloud to Taghi, '*A-tal, ma-tal, Too-too lay*', through the trees of the *marché provençal* where big, scrappy, yellow leaves littered the artists' empty stands. At the top of the market, Nasima pulled the pushchair into the secluded corner of a terrasse beside stacks of aluminium chairs and three-legged tables, and gave Taghi a bottle of fruit juice. Was everyone in the town watching the funeral from Paris? From where she sat beside Taghi's pram, she saw, on balconies and terrasses of the flats and old streethouses, the big polyps of satellite dishes forbidden in their own country. Wind blew round the ochre roofs, round the ancient turrets of the modern art museum. Everything smelt and tasted of boredom and, Khosro's word, 'rubbish'. *The aridity of a single cell living off itself*—a phrase Khosro had used to describe his past to her in their first weeks together, after her parents had left her behind with him. What did he mean? Why did he not speak their language so that she could understand? In the beginning Nasima had said to herself words didn't matter. He was overjoyed at the pregnancy. 'In my life you're like a garden of a thousand sunny greens after years in a dark room!' he told her, hiding his vehemence in her neck and hair, holding her tight to stop her drawing back to look puzzled into his face.

Oddly enough, alone in the leaf-strewn market, Nasima was missing Khosro. Who else had she to miss? In this marriage that had taken her through the mirror, she had lost her schoolfriends, her cousins. More gravely, she had thrown away the loyalty of her childhood alliance with Bahram. Perhaps the Khosro she was missing had never existed, perhaps it was only Nasima who had hoped to draw him out of that bone-thin, dark-faced boy-man who had played on the edge of her girl-hood ... the Khosro she had had in her mind would have been walking with her now, throwing stones in the windy sea for Taghi. They would have brought interesting things to eat and drink together, to shore up against the long, ugly day. That Khosro would not have abandoned her in this empty town without a word to put on the dullness she did not yet understand was boredom.

When they arrived back at the apartment, Khosro was still cross-legged in front of the TV. At Taghi's greeting he looked up, smiling quite normally, but then taking his son in his arms he began laughing hard, the way you do to deflate another person's self-importance. Taghi started writhing in protest. Over the baby's soft thin hair Khosro said, 'All those dead ashes piled honourably together! This is the highest point, the end-point of the social pyramid, a deadhouse!'

Nasima, looking at her husband, felt her heart contract with fear. How unshaven and pale he was! She exclaimed, 'You haven't eaten all day!'

He stared at her, pulled up short. His face was so pale under his unshaven beard that his dark eyes appeared to stain the skin below. Taghi began to cry hungrily, in earnest. Nasima took her baby from his father's arms and went off to the kitchen to make platefuls of food.

Thereafter, when Khosro's language began taking off on one of these incomprehensible flights she reacted in this way to calm him down. Her skilful, copious cooking of the dishes from their childhood was not an act of propitiation, or a trick like the honey her friends at home put in their babies' bottles to keep them asleep at night; it became a deep need, stirred by his words, that she could no longer stop in herself. Now she cooked busily, intently, undeterred even by Taghi's crying in the next room. The repetitiveness of cooking had henceforth a clearheaded compulsion to it, like the necessity to keep bailing out water gathering in the bottom of a wooden boat. Or maybe from her sauces, her chicken, fish, aubergines, green, red or black beans, from her dried lemons and apricots, her trays of *zaffron*-steaked rice, aromatic with dried vegetables and tiny red berries called *zirisch* whose tangy flavour soaked deeply on the tongue, she still hoped against hope to draw out of Khosro the Khosro that refused to be.

After Khosro had eaten his fill and cleared the dishes of food, the two of them sat closely together on the floor, backs to the wall. The baby played opposite them under the table. Khosro took a sugar cube in his teeth and drank his glass of tea through it, saying nothing. In moments like this he was speechless, thankful, borne along on his hopeless gratitude.

But his unhappiness was getting under her skin. She wouldn't have minded his distance from her, his exhausted absorption in his work, if only she knew he was content. Surely he needed to see people! At home, visitors to Europe had brought back video recordings of parties and celebrations, children's birthdays. Often she longed for Taghi to hear children playing in their own language. But Khosro had cut his ties with their people who had arrived with him in Europe, although this didn't stop him criticizing them as bitterly as if he had seen them that very day. If Nasima asked idly after such and such a person they had both known years ago, wondering if he or she were married, or how many children they had, Khosro embarked on a long, winding discourse to the effect that the political organization to which he had belonged had lost touch with the reality of life back there. 'They write pamphlets of ideological instructions! And not one of them can predict either the pattern of arrests today, or the people's reaction to them!'

What about contacts he had made here, in France? When she put the question to him Khosro reflected. He said that he would send off some postcards. Some people he knew might like a break in the south.

When discussions and telephone conversations had been under way for the marriage, Khosro himself had told her on the phone that for different periods, he had lived with two women in his years away. He said that he held particularly to telling her about his past, that these woman had meant as much to him as marriage partners. Luckily, Nasima's parents were out of earshot; Nasima begged Khosro not to mention anything to anyone in their town of these relationships. The least suggestion of this past would increase her family's fear for her and crush any possibility of their letting her go to him in France.

They had no family or friends to foster discussion but they still met through Khosro's daily translations of the television news. Before she understood that television made him worse, Nasima encouraged Khosro in these didactic commentaries which bored her as much as an attempt to read a book in a language she didn't understand. Out of the wordiness she had come to think of as the weavings of Khosro's overtired mind, only the images of Africa came swimming clear and nightmarish. In Africa that winter, the mud of overflowing refugee camps was stirred to infested slime by thousands of feet. A woman, introduced as Cecile, had a strong, masklike face, despite the sunken skin around the nose and one eye rolled in, dead from malnutrition. The only sign of her anguish was a long hand every now and then raised to her face in a gesture of disbelief. She had three children but had lost two in the panic of flight … but at the mention of children, Nasima turned her head away. Africa scared her. What was to stop the process which had transposed her from home to this place in France once more setting itself in motion and depositing her around those smoking campfires? She jiggled Taghi on her knee until, delighted, he pulled hard on a fistful of her hair, then squealed, drowning Khosro's rocking discourse, 'They are in the real world where the blood and all colours have dried to black and grey.'

Except he was wrong about it being only Africans who live in grey, thought Nasima, grimly. From day to day, the three of them lived in a colourless, unchanging haze, moving, in Nasima's case, from the indistinct outline of her husband's needs to those of her son. From day to day, their lives were losing substance, until they had as much, or less, impact on each other than the one-dimensional protagonists of the television news.

Then at last the real three-dimensional world burst in on them in the form of a letter from one of Khosro's old friends— neither of them would say 'lovers'—in Paris. Janie was coming to the south of France and would visit Khosro. Nasima found herself awaiting her eagerly. Her energy renewed, she cleaned all the rooms, laid in fruit, soft drinks and biscuits, and prepared a bed in Taghi's room, although Janie had not mentioned staying overnight. How good to have an opportunity to practise their hospitality! As she worked, enjoying the task of getting ready for a guest so much that she forgot the identity of the woman who was coming, Nasima talked to Taghi. 'People from our country', she told her son, 'are not meant to live alone.' Taghi grinned. Mother and son lived so much in the same skin that she did not have to describe it to him, she knew he had retained in detail the memory of her life in a house active with visitors, children, meals from six o'clock in the morning to two or three hours after midnight. Three storeys to clean, four brothers, two sisters-in-law and their children, an older cousin and her children—surely Taghi understood this unpeopled life with Khosro as nothing more than an intermission in their real, crowded lives, back there in that house in the flat, brown north of their country. Yet, having formulated this thought, Nasima obliterated it at once. It was too close to the belief she did not want to recognize in herself, the conviction that she and Taghi belonged elsewhere, that their separation from Khosro was inevitable.

After watching Janie for an hour, Nasima perceived that this woman understood Khosro's life, his melancholy, his marriage, more than Khosro himself. Thus Nasima, watching quietly at one corner of the table while Janie drank into her glass of tea and Khosro talked excitedly, understood more about this relationship of Khosro's with Janie than Khosro himself.

'Why do we talk so much?' Khosro broke off to gaze happily over Janie. Nasima made out her reply as something like, 'Oh, I've always this effect on people.'

Janie was keeping the tone very light. Unlike Khosro, she was aware of Nasima's watchful eyes and was hiding her pleasure in Khosro's company. She didn't know that Nasima was so glad to see Khosro happy she didn't care about jealousy. Anyway, when Nasima had set eyes on Janie, she had been relieved at once. This woman was not attractive. Only the whiteness of her skin would have excited admiration at home. She was fat and milky, with orange hair cut into a thick crest and orange freckles, and she was dressed like a man in flapping trousers and a bulky denim jacket. Nevertheless, as soon as she began talking back to Khosro, she startled Nasima by speaking with confidence that she had never seen even in a beautiful woman of her age.

'Janie always overimpresses people in the beginning,' Khosro said later. Janie talked—how she talked! Khosro, caught up in what she was saying, made no attempt to translate and began to roll a cigarette. A slight tremble in his hands reminded Nasima of the fear in the friendliness of his first smiles in the days following her parents' arrival in France for the marriage contract. But then, in the flow of Janie's words, Khosro forgot his fear. He was thinking, listening, biting back his disagreement or ejaculations of approval to keep on listening. From a beetle-shaped ashtray Nasima had brought with her from the bazaar in their town, he picked up a crumpled bus ticket, and as the other woman talked on and held him back several times from answering, he began folding the ticket precisely, tearing it into tiny bits. For a few minutes Nasima watched this folding, pressing process on the bus ticket between Khosro's fingers. Then she stood up, smiling, and went to console Taghi who was moaning in his cot, disgruntled at Nasima's unusual lack of attention. From then on that evening, Nasima came and went quietly from the table. At each visit to their conversation, she sat still at her place on the table corner for a few minutes, and then she moved, refilling teapots and emptying ashtrays. All the time, instead of looking at their faces, she looked at the progressive wearing down of the bus ticket in Khosro's fingers and the thin brown line down the middle of that oblong of yellow paper. Looking back, she had no memory of Khosro's face that evening. Nor did she remember the room around them, which must have been stuffy as usual with the smell of the old people's cooking seeping up from the downstairs flats and stale cigarette smoke and all the unwashed dishes from their dinner in the kitchen. It was as if Khosro's fingers clumsily folding and tearing the ticket had eclipsed all sensation, all perception.

Janie stopped and lit a cigarette. Khosro glanced up at Nasima and, to show Janie he practised sexual equality as much at home as in theory, went to the kitchen to make tea. Janie sat on, smoking and tipping her ash into the beetle-shaped ashtray. She caught Nasima's calm eye on her and admired the patterned seat of the chair vacated by Khosro. Haltingly, Nasima explained that the pattern and colours of the material were Kurdish. People in their town could buy Kurdish kilims and material in the mountains nearby for a few hundred francs, whereas in Europe this patch of hand-woven fabric would cost fifty times more. Khosro came back from the kitchen with a teapot and three glasses. The subject of the Kurdish cushion cover was not extended to that endless conversation of their people in exile that consisted of comparing prices over there and here in France. Nasima drank her tea and waited, concentrating. They were talking about unemployment in the little industrial towns near Belgium. 'The children of immigrants are angrier, much angrier than their parents,' she heard Janie say. Would Taghi then feel more violent than Khosro now launching excitedly into a tirade about singers in prison at home? She stifled a yawn and sat back and watched, threading through the ends of her long dark hair fingers that were sticky with the apples she had fed Taghi that afternoon ... Her head spun with listening to so much of another language and with keeping her eyes on their faces, as if her very intentness might make her understand. She had been up with Taghi since six o'clock that morning and when she left the table again to check on his breathing and adjust the mosquito net, the smell of his sleep, the quiet, overcame her, so that she nearly sank her head on the pillow beside him.

'What was she saying?' she demanded of Khosro the following day when Khosro came back from work. Janie had left by car for Nice in the middle of the night. Khosro was too tired to hear her; he yawned and then, catching her question, started laughing to himself, as if Janie had reminded him of something very funny.

'She said … she said that everyone has problems with the past. Reactionaries are constipated and revolutionaries have diarrhœa,' he said, his shoulders shaking in the mirthlessness she hated, and repeated himself, 'Reactionaries … constipated … and revolutionaries … diarrhœa …'

'And now?' Nasima asked herself.

When Khosro did not make himself available to her, she nearly hated him for his apparent indifference to her desire, this infidelity to her pale body that had grown thin and familiarly girlish again after childbirth and that she stretched in sleep beside him. His oblivion to her was a mockery of all those years of talking to her friends and cousins, all that thinking and waiting in the same house as her brothers while the girls she had gone to school with got married to doctors and engineers and Nasima's mother went on putting aside equipment for her kitchen and her first baby and worrying about her happiness. Nasima was furious with Khosro. All along, all those childhood afternoons, those rainy days and special occasions, the stretches of loneliness, or sickness, the sun slanting in through the windows of rooms had been leading to *this*, this incapacity of Khosro's for her, his feeble, turned head and his thin, pursed lips. Sometimes her anger was at herself, for where, in what mundanities of her life, had she read the transformation she had believed in? In what pattern of tea leaves, or morning frost? In the ink of a new book? Or the faint scent like talc from her own clothes hanging in the wardrobe ... all of it an empty dream, a narcissistic dream, for he wouldn't look at her. She couldn't bear sensing him avoid contact with the side of her body or the length of her hair on the pillow. Finally she got up to go into the other room and sat on the sofa until she fell asleep.

In the mornings after these restless nights, Nasima woke up dog-tired and lay unmoving, listening to Taghi having a conversation with the cloth picture she had hung on the bars of his cot. As soon as the baby sensed she was awake, he stopped. The sounds grew urgent, imperative; without taking the thumb out of his mouth he summoned his mother. He hated having his arms pushed through the sleeves of his jumpers and his cry as Nasima pushed and pulled was a cry of pure tragic loss. Then the sun rising up from the sea threw light on the clumped blue-green vegetation of the distant foothills, and crept slowly over blocks of flats and terraces, right up to the white façade of the block of flats opposite. Mist rose from the wet grass and the ancient trees planted in rows in the villa gardens. Even the winter days were still warm enough for the baby to play from two o'clock onwards in the sunshine on the balcony. Nasima sat and watched him, and watched the sun on the house roofs whose ochre glow contrasted the sunlit white of the house façades and the hairy trunks of the palm trees.

Her afternoons were not so busy now. She accomplished her days with the languor suited to what Khosro called 'the tail end' of the season on the Côte. 'The weather will soon get worse,' he promised, the only promise, thought Nasima, he had ever made them.

Maybe he had worked too much in his life and the fatigue of this work would kill him. He needed extra hours of sleep because, he said, even in sleep his brain kept up too much with its daily routine of finding formulae and solutions for his research to fall properly unconscious. When he came home from work now, Khosro reached for sleep as others reached for a glass of wine, a cigarette, or a musical instrument. Sometimes, pleading exhaustion, he ignored their bed and slept all night in a bundle in the corner of his room, as beggars sleep, back to the wall, knees pulled up to their chests. Often he accompanied his sleep discreetly upright, face concentrated, as if listening to distant conversation, or far-off music. Or he sat cross-legged, his feet folded out of sight under his thin behind, after a good meal. Once, Khosro came back from work and sat thus on the floor, head back against the wall, eyes half closed, and Nasima put it to him that he had worked too hard all his life, even in his days at school in their town. At this, Khosro opened his eyes and with his head still back on the wall chuckled, 'Yes, oh yes, that school in the *al-hashabi* district. Your brother Bahram was in my class. We're a fine subtle lot who graduated from *al-hashabi*, aren't we? After the years of torture they imposed on us! The workload!'

His mockery would have irritated Nasima if the sharpness in his eyes hadn't worried her. She had remembered one of

Bahram's insinuations on their father's initial contact with Khosro's family. 'Those that left the country after the repression began', said Bahram, 'weren't "mentally sound".' At the time, Nasima had not paid her brother's remarks much attention. Traditionally, older brothers expressed suspicion of the man who succeeded in negotiating marriage with their sister. For Bahram, this brotherly right to criticize was redoubled by the fact that Khosro would take his sister away from the place where she had grown up, not simply into another town, or to the capital where surely she would learn to despise her family, but to another country where she would forget her language and her religion!

'If we had a holiday, at *al-hashabi* they went out of their way to spoil it by giving us enormous, meaningless feats of homework to achieve, swearing to make our lives hell if we came back,' Khosro was saying. 'Write out the works of Hafez three times! Learn the first half of the Koran by heart! Just what you need for a kickstart in life, eh? What's with Bahram these days after his kickstart? Still working in his father-in-law's abbatoir? Wringing chicken necks and cooking the accounts?' When Khosro picked up some of Nasima's longing to talk about their town and the people they knew back there, he could go on like this all evening, laughing sourly to himself at unfunny anecdotes that grew more savage and unfunnier in the telling. A man who daubed slogans against the régime got his face rubbed along the wall until the cheek and jawbones showed through! A boy sent to the front during the war had sent home a photo of a body and head decapitated in a bomb blast to show people what was really happening, and a week later he was blown to pieces himself! A joke about political prisoners' counting the days—as if the length of time they had been in prison made any difference to their sentence! Nasima did not know where he would have stopped if it hadn't been for Taghi, who had learned to sit up and who cried angrily for his father's attention and then cried again when Khosro picked him up hungrily and squeezed his round, bald head against his own, muttering intensely, 'daddy's little darling, little heart, my little life, I don't deserve you do I, I know I don't deserve you, or your mother'.

Yet despite his contrition, Khosro now got angry when he felt Nasima's eyes on him not understanding his discontent. In the middle of the night he got up, irritated, from the mattress on which they both slept, lit a cigarette and sat bonily cross-legged on the floor, his back straight as his grandfather's against the wall, his thin mouth compressed. Nasima lay with her eyes squeezed shut, resisting Khosro's angry, imprisoned gaze in the dark, and also not giving in to a quality in him she associated with his slender ankles, his naked feet, twisted after childhood years of ill-fitting shoes. Imagining his bare feet on the floor, the tender closeness of the weak toenails cut carefully on the rounded ends of his long toes, always touched her unbearably, made her sit up, shake the sleep out of her eyes.

'What's the time? What're you doing there, Khosro?'

The trick was to pretend sleep and incomprehension.

'Thinking.'

The end of his cigarette burned through the thin dark. Nasima got up and sat beside him, her back against the dusty wallpaper. To counterbalance his burning-eyed clarity, she feigned sleepiness, as if the cigarette after cigarette he smoked lulled her senses instead of making her head ache, as if his unhappiness affected her no more than a fly buzzing for a way out against a closed window. In the next room, Taghi slept on his back. Outside, lights trembled from the yachts and the empty quaysides, on the deserted seafront road to Nice, on the black surface of the Mediterranean. Even in the deadest centre of the night, these lights on the shore cast a fuzzy orange halo on the black sky so that the dark was never total as it was at home. 'There must be a way,' thought Nasima, but the sentence remained unfinished in her head. She meant that if she talked like Janie, then she would know how, gradually and persistently, like polishing the reflection back into a tarnished mirror, to talk Khosro back into talking. But she had nothing to say. She sat on and on against the wall, listening for changes in Taghi's sleep in the other room and bearing with Khosro's unhappiness, and when the air turned into pigeon-coloured dawn they fell asleep together on the floor from exhaustion, just before Taghi woke them with his cries of hunger.

During the marriage negotiations, Bahram, who had been in Khosro's class at school, had been able to provide the family with details of the circumstances in which Khosro had left the country after the revolution. At the *lycée*, said Bahram, Khosro had been no more or less politicized than he. Only Khosro's reputation as a model student had made their revolutionary cell elect Khosro to denounce their teacher, a spy for the régime, in front of the class. In the moment that Khosro had stood at the blackboard and screamed his denunciation, all control ('respectfulness in anger' said Bahram pointedly, for Nasima's benefit) gave way to a tremor visible from head to foot, fusing fear and anger. The teacher was stolid, girthy, wirily moustached. He had sneered at the trembling young boy, his former star pupil, and ordered him to write a verse from the Koran on the board, so that he could ridicule his shaking hands.

The screaming denunciation had the desired effect. A week later, the teacher had left their town and was rumoured to have paid a 'passer' for a visa to Germany. Then Khosro had become too visible. Someone in their class was furnishing lists of names. A wave of arrests and executions was building in the town. (All this happened when Nasima, a little girl, was playing in their courtyard at feeding her doll with bricks.) The organization to which Bahram and Khosro and everyone else at school belonged then scraped and borrowed to get Khosro out of the country. No sooner had Khosro arrived in France, said Bahram, contemptuously, in the tones of the trader who sees only too well through another's fraud, than he dropped all political activity and concentrated on studying for a university degree. 'We don't even know if he ever paid back the money they spent to save his life. Who knows how he's living over there? And how come it's only now he's earning enough to get married?'

Shortly after they moved to the south of France, Bahram telephoned Nasima because he was worried by a series of television programmes depicting the discrimination and poverty endured by those who lived in 'self-imposed exile'. Why could Nasima not persuade her husband to come back to a life 'of comfort and self-respect' among his own? Khosro, who was aware of her brother's hesitations, related to Nasima how he had gone to a demonstration against the régime organized by the opposition in exile outside the embassy in Paris. There among the hunger-strikers on the pavement he saw the 'class-mate' from their town who had denounced him. The denouncer had himself been denounced and then escaped abroad in his turn.

'Bahram does not understand how people who spend their lives for an idea suffer too, in their own way,' said Khosro. 'He doesn't believe in the reality of their pain, their loneliness. I am telling you this because oddly enough I too may come, in a different, more roundabout way, to Bahram's cynicism. That crowd of protesters, their slogans have dissolved for me into the same grey. How many of them are someone else's minions, how many of them worth a life?'

She must bring herself to think of divorce, introduce with their families the idea of their separation. Taghi, his son, was of a beauty irrelevant to the obscene funniness of this man's ironizing to himself, night after night, into exhaustion. Now when Nasima walked the town, the *marché*, the cobbled ramparts under a winter sky so intensely blue it was nearly purple, she was looking for a way out, a way to get away from this marriage in Antibes … and then she was in luck. One Saturday morning a letter arrived from her mother. For months now Khosro's grandfather, he of the caravanserai, had been dying of a tumour of the colon. Khosro's family did not want to tell him. Nothing could be done; they did not want Khosro to suffer needlessly until the Haj died. Nasima knew her mother hoped she would tell Khosro, the favourite grandson, who might then drop everything and come back home to see the old man before he died.

Khosro usually spent most of Saturday asleep.

Her mother's letter in hand, Nasima waited for him to wake up. Her heart beat hard at the thought of going back with Taghi to their town, to the house where she had grown up. 'We're going home, home!' she whispered excitedly at the baby, who flexed the tip of his tongue and blew bubbles. She gave him a pocket mirror, out of the clutter of cheap paraphernalia that her mother had tearfully pressed on her in the airport at that last minute nearly two years ago—a selection of key-holders, key-rings, mini-purses, what Khosro called *bazaar kitschery*, all decorated with the same painted woman's face with long curved black hair and pointed eyes from the classical miniatures.

In sleep, tension or fear turned Khosro's olive skin yellow and tautened his fine lips to a pinched line, as if his mouth were a toothless hole. Watching Khosro curled up in the corner of the room, his face pale and his mouth tight and yellow, she thought, *he disgusts me, I can't bear to be near him anymore*, but the same sentence in her head ended guiltily, *he's so gentle, he'll never attack me directly*, and even gave way to a tremor of grateful relief at the memory of another face, sallow with sun and knowingness and eyes flicking over her like the tongue of some muscular animal.

'You're the first face that I know so well asleep,' she said to him, tenderly. Although she had spoken lightly, a tumultuous feeling came over her. Then she realized that behind his shut eyes Khosro was awake and had heard what she said. He didn't try to look at her. Quiet surrounded them where they sat opposite each other, and a minute later she sensed he had gone back to sleep again. Nasima was on the sofa, where Taghi too fell asleep peacefully, sweating through his hair onto her knee. She thought of how she had grown immune to the ugliness of this room, which had so disappointed her the first time she had entered and smelt the deadness from the carcasses of furniture. The months of their living here had displaced the musty damp, but the air remained dim and stuffy. In their country, the windows of dwelling places looked into private courtyards, the houses always turned blind walls to the streets, and Nasima felt too exposed to open the long panes or pull back the netting on the windows during the day.

Towards the middle of the afternoon, Khosro stumbled awake, blinking tiredly after the dark of his sleep, yawning before he noticed her waiting on him. In those moments of his awakening, she saw him as the bone-thin, violent-eyed boy-man of her girlhood, whose force of feeling transformed the puckishness of his narrow face with its long nose, small forehead and straight, heavy eyebrows. She feared his sensitivity. He had a way, when he was half awake, of holding his elbows, hunching his shoulders, that reminded her of a starving child or an old man in a cottage doorway. A terribly thin, sharp-eyed slave boy. And so she said nothing to him of the letter.

Pity had stopped her speaking. But from then on, Khosro's policy of never talking about their town, never asking after her family or the people she had left behind, angered her unbearably. To think that before their marriage she had imagined he wanted a girl from their town and not some European, so that he could talk about the place where they had both grown up! In the very beginning he had listened to her, smiling, when she talked, but never adding anything himself, and now if she did not make an allusion to the town or their families, all that previous life might never have existed at all. One time only could she remember Khosro referring spontaneously to the world where they had spent their childhood. On a trip to a village inland at the beginning of their time in Antibes, big, black crows alighted cawing on a ploughed field, and Khosro shivered and said, 'How I hate that noise!' It reminded him of Fridays at home, the day of family and prayer, when in the becalmed, dusty silence came the cawing of birds, rooks or big blackbirds from trees in the enclosed backyards. Khosro's involuntary shiver of distaste disturbed Nasima. If he hadn't married her to recover the flavour of his origins, and if she couldn't bring him back in imagination to his own country, what else could she offer him? Khosro had gone on talking, abstractedly as usual, of the destruction of the French peasantry, and his endless, curling stream of words wound round and round her while her fear circled intolerably higher and higher.

'But what do you miss about back there?' she cried, more indignantly than she had intended.

He looked at her, startled into one of his flashes of tenderness.

'Watermelons.' He said slowly, 'How we cooled them in the backyard pool in summer.' He looked at her face and added, 'The white dust on the roads. That peppery fine dust, that powders the walls and roofs of houses.'

The wind had begun to blow hard in their faces off the Mediterranean. Offended at his just saying the first thing that came into his head, she didn't look at him, she kept her eyes down and arranged Taghi's quilt tighter around his head to protect him from the wind and so that she didn't have to look at her husband.

She no longer followed his many words into the long sentences they made up. She felt as if she had heard it all before and knew exactly what he would say, and in the strain of listening again to his descriptions and conclusions, the loneliness and tiredness of the whole day of shopping and cleaning and cooking and playing with Taghi rose in her bones. Khosro, like Nasima, was apparently moving towards some crisis point, and although like her he would never attack outright, he began hinting that he too had cause to feel some lack in her. In the same way as words of French now separated themselves from the babble in the shops and the television, Nasima began to take in the meanings unwinding from Khosro's long discourses, including the facile philosophizing which was the nearest he would come to discussing the failure of their marriage.

'Desire is not love, the desire to love is not enough to love. The will to be happy does not make happiness. Love is not always shared as it should be.'

On the other side of the ramparts that day, the sea was as smooth as a child's cheek. In the pushchair, Taghi's head drooped in sleep. Nasima had spent all morning playing with him in the sandpit at the *jardin d'enfants*. Khosro touched his son's head, sighed and ran on idly, sifting through words as if letting sand run through his fingers.

'There are so many different forms of love, none of them can be ordered to size. Only rarely can they be made to reciprocate.'

So he knew too. But she would have to be the first to speak to their families. She put it off to after Christmas, partly because she wanted to send cards to her cousins and school-friends who envied her and who in their letters had quoted 'Happy Christmas' and asked for details of Christmas celebrations. In the darkening afternoons she lingered with Taghi among the red and green decorations, the snow sprayed in corners of shop windows, the smell of the bakeries, the shops bursting with goods, fruitbreads, trays of oysters, and the fruit of the region, kumquats, pyramids of little oranges, lemons, dark bottles of wine. Now she was adept at excluding the pain of knowing that if Khosro were with them, his comments, his *there-is-a-decadence-in-this-elaborate-attention-to-appearance-expresses-a-triteness-a-desuetude-that-is-really-the-centre-of-an-old-decaying-culture*, would have separated her from the air of festivity that made her feel at home and also full of longing.

After Christmas, she would have to formulate the words to tell her married cousin about the end of her marriage. Her cousin would find a way to let her parents know.

Then a letter arrived from Bahram.

Details of the worsening economic situation in their town made up the first part of his letter. Last year, Bahram's wife Maryam, pregnant with their second child, had had a fetish for oranges. This year oranges were not available except at the price of a week's salary for one kilo on the black market and what if Maryam fell pregnant again? Bahram had taken on another accounts job four evenings a week to make ends meet ... The second part of the letter, given over to the traditional fraternal sentiment of loss on his sister's marriage, revealed that enough time had elapsed for Bahram to enter into an equally traditional stage of personal criticism of the man for whom 'she had left her country and family'. The brother of the man from whom he and his wife rented their apartment, had, like Khosro, 'chosen to quit' the country when 'events here took on a more catastrophic turn'. He lived in Los Angeles, where, everyone said, the situation was better for exiles than in Europe. Had she never wondered at Khosro's extraordinary luck in getting out of the country when events soured? Never asked why, of the names blacklisted by informers, Khosro was among the few to get a visa to the Eastern bloc and from there to make his way westwards? A lot of members of Khosro's revolutionary student movement were coming out of prison now, after their years of suffering which Khosro had spent as a student in Europe. Most of them, like Bahram, were managing to make ends meet by setting up market stands in food or household utensils and putting behind them the fact that they were working elbow to elbow with the *bazaaris* they once despised. Their landlord's brother in Los Angeles sent home his family-in-law two hundred dollars a month.

When Nasima came to this sentence, with the two hundred dollars standing out as the clumsy nub of the whole letter, her eyes skipped over the final paragraph's standard inquiries after Taghi and usual requests for photos. Calmly she folded the page of her brother's writing and, wanting to put it someplace where, without throwing it in the bin, she could forget she had ever received it, she placed the pages firmly in the centre of a book Khosro had left on the table. Taghi, sitting on the floor at her feet and chewing wetly on a plastic brick, saw the anger and shame of this gesture at once. He dropped his brick and began calling imperiously at the book until Nasima lifted him and carried him over to another corner of the room. She arranged a circle of toys around him, then came back to the table where she had left Khosro's book with the letter. It was a heavy tome—a religious book? The title, from what Nasima could make out from a design of interlocking purple and white cubes, was scientific. *Molecular disorder ... and problems of fission.* What did it mean? At the same time the soundlessness of the words in her head seemed to distil their meaning; she had known words like that before in their own language. Words from the television and radio that left a rustle on the surface of the skin they wanted to penetrate, *nest of spies, snakes in the dark. In the quest for justice, family will divide against family, the children against their father, sister against brother, husband against wife* ... Nasima frowned and took the letter out of the heavy book so that Khosro would not read it. What had she been thinking of? she reprimanded herself. Letter in hand, she went into the kitchen to start cutting celery and chicken for the night's meal. Laughing wildly, Taghi followed her on his hands and knees. In the midst of the cooking, the folded square of letter was left on a shelf for its comments to be forgotten amid the previous tenants' old grease stains that Nasima had not managed to scrub away.

Later that afternoon, after the lunch and evening meal had been prepared and Taghi, woken up from his post-lunch nap, was shrieking as she tickled him, Nasima sat back on her heels, puzzled by a quiet underneath the traffic noises from the open balcony windows and Taghi's squirms and bubbly screams of delight. Then she understood. It was from Bahram's letter that this stillness had spread inside her. Rather than re-read her brother's words aloud to Taghi or rush excitedly to write her answer, stumbling out her sentences and careful with her spelling, she had for the first time put Bahram aside. Using the calm that came naturally to her, she had hushed her anger at that voice in his letter. With a sudden apprehension of that self always described by others as gentle, tactful, Nasima looked at her long, strong, brown hand with its manicured nails on her son's body. If Bahram's voice, the voice of home, was to go quiet, then this self in its timidity and gentleness was all that was left to her.

Out of the early morning rain after Khosro left for the laboratory, a grey, metallic mist came off the sea two or three streets
away, off the humps and ribs of the mountains it floated
vaporously, as if out of dragons' lairs. Christmas over, the
shoppers had abandoned the streets to sweeping grey veils of
rain, from the lamp-posts steel stars clanked into unlit gar-
lands of festive bulbs that apparently no one wanted to take
down. In the evenings wind beat around their house, like the
grey sea tossing a ship on its surface, so that Nasima was afraid
but didn't cry. She was getting used to not shedding tears when
she was sad or afraid. Once, watching a film about war in
Europe, she saw trains taking prisoners away, and when the
train was standing at a siding in an isolated village a woman
leaned out and abandoned her baby on the rails in the hope
that someone would come along and save it. Nasima huddled
over on the sofa-bed where Khosro had curled up to sleep on
that first night, and waited to weep desperately along with the
lusty cries of the abandoned baby on the railway track. But her
eyes remained dry, Taghi woke up and Khosro came home.

'*A-tal, ma-tal, Too-too lay*'

'Too-tay!' Taghi now shouted.

People smiled less at Taghi when she pushed him across
town in his pram. He was no longer a newborn. He now refused
to wear his pixie hat, preferring to hold it in his hand over the
side of the pram and wait for a moment to drop it under other
people's feet. Every day, Nasima sensed his ability to resist sickness, to play and eat and sleep well, his taking on life and the
rhythm of life as his unquestioned right. His head had lost the
bald, European look. Dark silky hair grew long over his ears,

smelling of warm sleep and the sweetness of the special sham-
poo she walked across town to get from a Tunisian shop.

She had learned to live in the interim between the present
and some future resolution to leave and take Taghi back home.
Apart from the divorce decision itself and the shock waves of
its officialization at home, there would be material and practical ramifications which Nasima did not know if she could
count on Khosro to help her resolve. She understood this
when after a night of rain she was standing at the window,
Taghi in her arms, and watching the tramp in the bricked-up
villa below. He had stopped reading to lift up the lumps of
cardboard that hung over the balcony and was examining them
for dry parts.

'We could leave him some food, when he's not there,' she
murmured, 'or warm clothes.' How did the old man get
through the long hours when the street lamps went out and it
was too dark to read?

'Food!' Khosro said scornfully, 'He doesn't need food, or
clothes. There are organizations here that supply him with all
that. It's money he's in need of. You have to leave him money
to buy what he likes. Medicines. Or alcohol.'

He shrugged at the shudder she gave this last word. His
dismissiveness annoyed Nasima. He knew that she hadn't got
money of her own to give anyone. How to get money for a
divorce? What if Khosro got too sick to work and the three of
them ended up on some balcony behind a sodden lump of
cardboard? She had considered working in one of the shops in
town where her gentleness and mild manners would win her
smiles from the elderly customers. But for that she would have
to speak more of the language, the knowledge of her working
would have to be kept from her family, and who would look

after Taghi in the hours she was away? Any prospect of earning money had to be put off until Taghi began school ...
When the wind blew round the castle of Picasso's paintings,
she no longer thought of Khosro's caravanserai and its sand-
blown courtyards, the well hundreds of years old which smelled
of cold dust but still gave water. If she went back there now, she
would be afraid of the hardy desert animals, the birds of prey
and rodents inhabiting the buildings. *If they went back* ... she
didn't like to think of Taghi as one of the shaven-headed
schoolboys who swarmed after the tourists taking buses out of
town to look around the desert.

Going back was suddenly out of question for the time being.
On the other side of the border to the south of their town back
home, a war had begun. Abruptly, in a single movement not
unfamiliar to Nasima, nor even to Khosro after his ten years
away, their particular unhappiness was subsumed in a general
ambiance of fear. *'It's beautiful, it's opening up like a Christmas
tree, like fairy lights,'* cried the pilot of a bomber out of Khosro's
rickety black and white portable from the sky over the capital.
Khosro, sitting on a straight-backed chair, his legs decorously
crossed, explained that the lights over the city came not from
the bombs themselves but from special reconnaissance flares
meant to light up ground-level targets. They watched TV, listened to the radio, translated newspapers for allusions to the
war. Khosro called her from work to ask what she had heard
and to pass on news. In the evenings, Taghi crawled over to the
screen, stood up and changed channels to get their attention.
Their town in the north escaped untouched, apart from the
young men, some of Khosro's cousins called up to the front.

When the war was over, Nasima did not need to receive a letter from Bahram to understand that food shelves in the shops
were empty, the hospitals empty too of medicines but full of
the injured. There was talk of cholera. Everywhere, the régime
was arresting students, dissidents, spies, to bite off in the bud
any criticism or blame for the war now lost. For the foreseeable
future Nasima had to forget going back.

The fear generated by the war softened their disappointment in each other, and reminded them, if not of the 'garden
of a thousand sunny greens', of their long-ago gratitude for the
shelter they had found in this marriage. In the evenings,
Khosro left the TV and took to playing with Taghi in the
kitchen while Nasima, smiling to herself, prepared dinner. He
began commenting once more on how much the baby resembled Nasima. 'His hands are replicas of yours,' he said, adding
shamefacedly, 'and he never makes others unhappy either, he's
like you that way too.' Taghi had stopped his long screeches
and played at emitting a high-pitched tone as softly as possible with great concentration, so that Khosro and Nasima
looked at him in astonishment. 'Little burnt father!' swore
Khosro under his breath. For a time, the renewal of their pride
and surprise at Taghi made the warmth and light of the flat
into the centre of the world. The town outside in its winter
weather, the terror of the war raining its fairy lights back
home, all that had dominated them became no more than a
backdrop to the uniqueness of their son.

Spring was still a long way off. They were living out an
interminable winter of warm, brown rain. Occasionally, in a
window of sunny weather, the sea turned shiny blue and talked
to itself on the sand that sparkled like snow where Nasima
took Taghi to play. Even if Nasima ever went home and ever

married again (unthinkable! even if she lived in the capital), never would she forget these days of pushing Taghi through these little cobbled streets of antique dealers and perfume shops, never forget the surgically clean bakeries where the mirrored surfaces and glass tops contrasted with the voluptuous perfection and artistry of the cakes. France. This was France. Once, waiting on a bench for Taghi to finish his bottle, she witnessed an old man, thin with white hair and pale blue eyes, clutching his blue packets of Gauloises as he came out of a *tabac*, shout at one of the tramps, a younger man, black-haired, crouching on the side of the pavement. 'Go home,' he shouted, '*espèce de fada!*' Turning to Nasima, the old man said, 'They are a lot more abusive here than they would dare back in their own countries! They know rightly back home they'd be got rid of once and for all!' *Yes, yes, he's right*, Nasima was thinking behind the soft smile she gave nearly everyone in town, *back home misfortune is a plunge without return over the precipice … if you fall under the wheels of the machine there you'll be mashed to pieces.* Looking down at Taghi's round head, the image came again of the dented, fly-blown diesel-powered bus out of town with the other tourists laughing at the hard, shaven-headed little boys of five or six leaping on and off to hand the women in like strong little men as the bus roared and shook along. From then on, she turned away from those who even looked like potential beggars or homeless, the quiet, solitary old people in smelly thick winter coats and scarves in warm weather, or the talkative, greasy-haired ones of all ages.

In the evenings, the landscape and foothills darkened to deep blue through a frosty mist. The radio said that on the other side of the mountains so much snow had come that the ski stations were closed. After Taghi went to sleep, spectacular skies shone for an hour above the dark, coldbound land, angel's cheeks, opalescent and pink shores, reaches of pure faint yellow in which long, dark purple clouds drifted near the land. Nasima watched these slow clouds until they disappeared. They were like fish. Long friendly fish that warmed her heart for they turned the land and the sky into an underwater world, comforting in its slow rhythm. The skies diminished the mountains, they sank into shadow and when the brightness faded and cleared to pale blue, the mountains rose again in silhouette. There, between the rise to the summit and the broad plains running to the shore, the lights of towns and villages winked their elves' eyes in the purple cold. In the dead middle of the night, Nasima had to get up out of bed for Taghi. Over the silent streets, with their big metal Christmas stars of dead bulbs clanging on the lamp-posts, arched a black sky dense with stars, shimmering and static. *All the souls ever born and ever to be born.* Living with Khosro had filled her mind with phrases like that. *There is no death there is only me who is going to die.* Solemn, she stared, at the diagonals, the lightly wreathed clumps ... Tonight, at least, this patterned, halted sky must lull the dispersed and their children, the tramp with his book, as far south as the smoking African marshes, as distant as her family in their town under the terrible Christmas-tree lights of war extinguished for the time being ... there was no other way to live the days but for the time being ... On such nights, it was reassuring to add her sleep to that of Khosro and Taghi and dream that all over the world had come a return of that far-off motionlessness of childhood.